HER VAMPIRE ADDICTION

I vowed never to love again...

For over 1500 years, I've mostly walked alone. A vampire, a monster in the dark.

Until she walks into my club: a ray of sunshine in the blackest night.

She's blonde. Beautiful. Sassy. Submissive.
   And 100% human.

I'm a predator, and she's my perfect prey. I'll have her tied up and quivering as I give her pain and pleasure like she's never felt before.

But I'm not the only monster hunting her. And if I don't take her – claim her – I'll lose her forever...

HER VAMPIRE ADDICTION

TABITHA BLACK

MIDNIGHT ROMANCE, LLC

PREFACE

Click here to sign up for Midnight Doms news!

DEDICATION

For my heart.
I'll never look at roses the same way again.
Thank you for being my inspiration...

1

S abina

It's been over an hour, and I'm starting to rethink this whole sodding evening. The air is stiflingly hot, and it's not just my palms which are clammy as I tug once again at the dratted skirt which insistently rides up my thighs, even though I'm not doing anything but standing in line. The new heels I'm wearing are pinching my toes and making my calves ache, and while I do get off on pain in a variety of circumstances, enduring burning soles in the attempt to make my legs look longer is not high on my kink list. Some women wear high heels effortlessly. Unfortunately, I am not one of them.

Pushing a damp strand of hair off my face, I blow out a breath and stare at the bouncer's broad, suited back, willing him to turn and look at me, to finally let me into this club

I've heard so much about but never been allowed to attend. *Never until now*, I correct myself. The bouncer doesn't move.

All around me, people are making easy, casual conversation, almost as if they expected a long wait, and are impervious to the muggy evening air. After all, Club Toxic is currently the most happening destination in downtown Tucson, despite persistent rumors that some people have come here and never been seen again.

People do love to gossip.

While there's a whole bunch of us waiting in line like the kids who were always picked last for the team, every now and then, self-important individuals or small groups of people sweep right on by—most of them not even deigning to glance our way—and march confidently up to the two burly doormen who immediately step aside—if not deferentially, then at least respectfully. This has happened a few times since I've been standing here, and although I've checked repeatedly, I haven't yet been able to spot any kind of wristband or hand stamp or anything else to distinguish these obviously VIP guests from the rest of us.

What do they have that we haven't?

Glancing behind me, I see that dozens more people have since joined the queue, all dressed in their clubbing finery, all apparently content to stand forever in the oppressive Arizona heat just for a chance to... do what, exactly? Have a drink? Hang out with their friends? This is Tucson, there's no shortage of venues for a good night out. So why this one? What's so special about Club Toxic? Is it just the reputation? The rumors? Are they thrill-seekers, or merely desperate to be trendy?

I have an ulterior motive for being here, but even so, I've now made up my mind that if I don't get in within the next ten minutes, I'm going home. Whenever Zeke talked about this place, his lip curling into a sneer as he warned me to stay the fuck away, he never mentioned having to stand in line for hours first. That would have been more of a deterrent than anything else he could have told me.

Ironically, it was his casual hint that there might be a kink scene here which piqued my interest. We had been dating for a week or so, and discussing whether to go out—and where to—when I had suggested Club Toxic.

"Absolutely not," he'd said, his thick blond brows drawing together in a frown. "And you don't go there, ever."

"Why?" I'd asked him, genuinely baffled. It was the first time I'd seen him so aggressive.

"It's not just a nightclub. It's dangerous. I've heard things. Shit goes on in the basement... people getting up to all kinds of perverted stuff. There was recently a shooting outside. I don't want to discuss it. Just promise me you'll never go."

"I promise," I'd said, desperate to ask more questions but recognizing that it probably wasn't a good idea in his current mood.

Zeke. That asshole. As it turned out, that first display of thinly veiled belligerence was just the tip of the iceberg. I dumped him yesterday, after barely four weeks of dating. I don't need that kind of negativity in my life.

I don't need *anyone*.

Still, it was with a tiny, perverse sense of satisfaction that I got dressed up tonight and came out here—partly because I could really use a good play session, and partly because I know how furious Zeke would be if he knew. Not that I intend for him to find out.

It's been way too long since I was able to lose myself in that heady, intoxicating bliss of subspace. I don't know for sure whether there really is any kind of BDSM club in the basement, but I'd very much like to find out.

"You there! The blonde!"

It takes me a second to realize that someone's calling out to me and I turn to find the source of the gruff male voice. A tall man is standing on the other side of the velvet rope, a mere foot or so away, his piercing gaze directed at me. I raise a questioning eyebrow.

"Yes, you. Want to come in with me?"

Even though it's phrased as a question, there's an inherent hint of command in his inflection and I find myself obeying instinctively, ducking under the rope and moving towards him.

Some people just have that dominant tone which flicks my sub switch. Besides, this is my ticket inside. I'd be a complete fool to turn it down.

I'm no fool.

As soon as I reach the man's side, he grips my upper arm and steers me toward the doors, not even giving me a chance to examine him properly. No matter. If we don't get on, I can make my excuses and go explore by myself. I just have to get through the fucking door first.

"Allan. Liam." My new companion addresses the bouncers curtly as they step aside to let us through. A blast of arctic air-conditioning ruffles my hair as we head into the club proper.

The place is jammed with writhing, grinding bodies and the thumping, bass-heavy music makes it seem like a living thing, an entity with a powerful heartbeat controlling everyone inside.

"Drink?" my companion asks once we've passed the coat check booth.

"Name?" I counter, glad when he comes to a halt and looks down at me because now I finally have a chance to assess him. His dark hair flops over his smooth, pale forehead. He has a large, almost beaky nose and thin, unsmiling lips.

"Ethan," he says, his hand still possessively on my upper arm. And you are?"

"Sabina."

"It's nice to meet you."

He has a strange accent. I want to say British but not quite. Almost as if he's lived in a few different places. If I had to guess his age, I'd say mid to late thirties. Physically he's not really my type, but now that I'm actually inside the club, I'm not keen on the idea of wandering around alone just yet. "It's nice to meet you too. And I'd love a drink. Thank you."

Ethan steers me off to the right, to a huge, mahogany bar. All the stools are occupied and I curse inwardly. I had been hoping for a chance to give my sore, aching feet a break.

"Red wine?" he asks.

"Sure."

"Good choice." He turns back to the bar and I'm amazed at how fast he's served, considering the crowd.

While he organizes the drinks, I assess my surroundings. It's cooler than it was outside, but not by much, which is something I attribute to the sheer number of people crammed into the place. There's a lounge area to my right, beyond the L-shaped mahogany bar. The dance floor is directly in front of me. Couples are dancing, grinding up against one another to the point of dry-humping in places, but try as I might, I can't see any trace of anything even remotely kinky.

Shame.

"Here." Ethan's voice drags me back to the present and I accept the proffered glass gratefully.

"Thank you." I take a sip, savoring the sweet, full flavor. "This is nice."

His long, slender fingers are curled around the stem of his own glass as he brings it to his lips. "Lots of body," he says, then directs a penetrating, sweeping stare from the top of my head all the way down to my shiny mauve shoes. "Delicious."

Something about the way he says that makes me uneasy and I take another long swallow of wine to distract myself. Everything's fine. I'm in control. I can take care of myself. I'll finish my drink, thank him again, and be on my merry way.

Then his piercing grey eyes meet mine and he growls, so low I can barely hear it, "You like pain. I can give it to you."

Despite my surprise, I can't prevent the sudden tingle between my thighs or the way my breath catches in my chest. And for some reason, I find myself completely unable to lie.

"I do." It's more a croak than a whisper.

"You thought this was a BDSM club."

Is he reading my mind? "I had heard rumors. But it would seem I was mistaken." I want to look away from him but it's strangely impossible. Almost as if he's hypnotized me.

"What if I told you there was a place beneath our very feet where I could take you into a dark corner and hurt you in all the ways you crave... and some you don't even know you want—yet?"

"I'd say you're lying," I whisper, my heart pounding, my fingers rigid around the bulb of my wine glass.

His cruel mouth turns up in a mocking sneer. "Then drink up, and I'll prove I'm telling the truth."

A little voice in my head is screaming at me that this is not a good idea, that there's something inherently untrustworthy about him. But I'm also curious. And I can't deny the effect his words are having on me.

My eyes are burning but I'm unable to blink as I raise my glass to my lips once more and drink deeply, draining the wine in a few measured swallows.

"Sabina." The way he says my name... it feels almost like a caress. My mind is foggy as he sets our glasses down on the bar behind him and lays a bill beside them before turning back to me. His suit looks expensive. The effects of downing almost an entire glass of wine in one go kick in, a rush of giddy warmth spreading throughout my body and making me unsteady on my feet.

Ethan grips my upper arm once more and guides me back toward the coat check area. To my astonishment, we actually go into the booth and then through a hidden door. *It really is a secret entrance*, I find myself thinking.

As we descend what seems to be an interminably long staircase, he's crooning in my ear, "I'm going to make you feel so good. Things you didn't even know you were capable of. Just trust me."

Trust him? After ten minutes and one drink? He's obviously delusional, but I still murmur something agreeable because for one thing, my heart is pounding with excitement and for another, I'm now very curious to see where these steps lead.

We've finished our descent and I stop dead in my tracks, overwhelmed by the sight that greets me. "There really is a kink club down here," I breathe, almost to myself.

The place is bathed in a red glow and there's music here, too, but it's more sensual than upstairs. Directly opposite us is a bar, to our right is a huge dancefloor. A raised dais with what looks like two huge thrones on it has just caught my eye when, from behind me, Ethan cups my breast, digging his fingers in cruelly. I gasp and my head falls back against his shoulder.

"Let's go somewhere a little more private, hon," he rasps, and begins steering me expertly through the people on the dancefloor. I glimpse flashes of erotic activity—a naked brunette on her knees is sucking someone's cock; a slender young woman is bent over, wrapped around a sturdy man's hip, holding on to his ankles as he spanks her soundly—and then we're in some kind of booth.

"Disrobe." Ethan's voice is icy.

This is suddenly happening way too fast. I glare at him and once again, my limbs feel warm and heavy, my mind foggy. "Wait," I whisper.

"I'll count to three."

This is all wrong. I haven't actually agreed to scene with him. We haven't discussed limits, a safeword, preferences, nothing. I glance beyond his shoulder towards the rest of the club. There's a thick curtain but no door. Thank god.

"Eyes on me," he says. "One."

"Look, Ethan," I begin, deliberately using his name rather than *Sir* or any other term of respect. "This is happening too fast for me. Can we please go and have another drink, discuss things—"

"Two." He takes a step towards me. My palms are suddenly clammy again and I wipe them on my dress. "Trust me, you do not want to make me say *three*."

"Why?" I raise my chin defiantly. "Will you hurt me?"

His eyes are so strange. They looked grey earlier but now it's almost like there are violet rings in the irises. His slender face is taut with anger. "Three."

As Ethan lunges towards me, I sidestep him and make a break for the curtain, shoving the thick, velvety material aside, knowing now exactly how a fly must feel in a spider's web as I get tangled in it and struggle to free myself. "Help!" I scream, knowing nobody could possibly hear me above all the sounds of the club—the music, the conversation, the cries of pleasure and pain. "Help!"

There's a sharp, prickling pain at the base of my skull and I realize Ethan has wrapped my hair around his fist and is tugging me back into the booth. "Feisty little thing, aren't you?" he says coolly. I'm horrified by how casual he still is— and by his strength. I'm not one of those tiny, slender little women who look like a stiff breeze could carry them away. I'm tall. I have hips, and thighs. And I can fight. Been doing it all my life.

I'm still wondering how Ethan is overpowering me with such apparent ease when a loud tearing sound rents the air and I realize he's ripped my dress clean off my body, exposing me to his piercing gaze. His expression, as he wraps one hand around my throat and pinches my nipple cruelly with the other, is contemptuous. Mocking. "Oh dear," he says coolly. "I told you not to let me get to three."

2

—————

M *aximus*

SATURDAY NIGHTS ARE ALWAYS the busiest, but this one's even worse than usual. The line outside of people waiting to get in is longer than ever, and I'm grateful I'm on dungeon monitor duty tonight. It's too damn hot out there so there are too many bugs. Why Lucius had to pick Arizona of all places to settle is beyond me, but we're here now so we have no choice but to make the best of it.

Besides, there's always something. He turned me 1600 years ago. In that time, I've seen it all and done it all, and nothing is ever one hundred percent perfect.

A ragged gasp catches my attention and I look to the source of the sound. Some people might have trouble differentiating between the regular noises people make when they're engaging in BDSM, and the sounds they make when they're in some kind of trouble. I'm not some people. I do have a huge amount of experience, after all—not to mention very keen senses. I can literally hear a pin drop.

The gasp came from a pretty young thing with her top rucked down to expose her breasts. Clover clamps are affixed to both her nipples, crushing them in their vice-like grip, and Eddie is tugging at the chain to make them tighter, a grin of sadistic pleasure lighting up his face. The girl gasps again, a definite sound of pain, but her expression is calm, her hips writhing softly as if she were humping the air.

False alarm then.

I settle back onto my stool. It's tucked discreetly away in a corner between the private booths and the play stations, within hearing distance of pretty much everything right up to the bar. All the better for me to watch out for everyone.

A slender redhead struts by and for the briefest of seconds, I feel a pang in my chest where my heart used to beat. Caroline's hair was the exact same shade. Then I clench my fists and will the thought away. It's been over a century. I should be over it by now. I *am* over it.

Then why are you still atoning? a tiny voice in the back of my mind asks me insistently.

I'm not atoning for anything, I argue back. I just like to look out for people. The world is a dangerous place—I should know—and, especially in this day and age, there's not enough kindness. Chivalry. There aren't enough heroes.

There was a time when women were regarded as the precious, sweet, fragile creatures they are. When they were treated differently. Now, they strut around believing they're equal to men in every way. Certain they can handle themselves, regardless of what happens. I wish it were so, but all too often, they overestimate their abilities and someone has to step in and rescue them.

It might as well be me.

"Help!"

Immediately I'm off my stool, tense, alert, my mind automatically triangulating the direction of the sound. It was faint but plaintive, easy enough to catch. Then I hear it again.

"Help!"

Help is never a safeword. Within moments, I've reached private play booth number three and yanked the curtain back. "What's going on here?" I growl, immediately clocking the pretty blonde who's wearing nothing but a thong and high heels, and Ethan, who has one hand around her throat and one of her nipples between his thumb and index finger. The woman looks terrified.

"We're playing, Maximus," Ethan rasps. "Nothing to see here."

"Is that so?" I raise an eyebrow and address the woman directly. "Did you just call for help?"

A mortal might not have noticed the way Ethan's long fingers tightened ever so slightly around her slender pale throat. I'm not a mortal. The blonde remains silent but gives the tiniest nod of her head.

"Playtime's over, Ethan," I tell him. "Let her go. Now."

We stare at each other in that inherently male challenge of aggression men have been exchanging since the beginning of time. Ethan licks his lips and his gaze returns to his captive.

"I won't ask you again," I say.

The blonde whimpers as he releases her nipple, but his other hand remains on her throat.

"Sabina," Ethan croons, "please tell this gentleman that you're here of your own free will."

Her long, mascaraed eyelashes flutter as she fights to drag her gaze away from him and that's when I realize:

Ethan has her in his thrall. The fucker has compelled her, and even though she's obviously fighting it, she's no match. No human can ever completely resist a vampire's thrall.

"You son of a bitch," I growl. "You stop that right now, or I swear I will kill you." I can almost see the wheels turning in his head as he decides his next move. He knows I'd be happy to make good on my threat. Consent is a fluid thing in Club Toxic, but all vampires who enter are well aware that using their thrall to coerce humans into doing their bidding is not something that is ever taken lightly.

With a pathetic huff, like a dog whose bone has been torn from its jaws, Ethan releases the girl's throat. Her knees immediately give way and she sinks to the floor like a ragdoll. I don't think, I just act, blurring to her side and catching her just before she hits the ground, well aware that Ethan will use that opportunity to escape.

Sure enough, by the time I'm kneeling beside the blonde, cradling her in my arms, the fucker's gone. No matter. I'll deal with him later. Once Lucius hears of this, he'll be happy to give me permission.

The blonde is staring vacantly up at the ceiling, her eyes glazed, her waterfall of silky hair cascading over my arm. And even though my protective instinct is now in full swing, her expression is so like the one she'd be wearing if I'd pushed her to the edge of bliss, her skin is so soft and warm, and her pert breasts are pointing so deliciously to the sky that I can't help but feel myself harden.

Her scent is a tantalizing mixture of fear, fresh sweat, and expensive perfume. There's also an underlying tinge of arousal, and I find myself wondering what the fuck Ethan did to get her to accompany him down here in the first place. Even more strangely, the thought of him giving her any kind of pleasure makes me madder than the knowledge that he hurt her.

What had he called her? *Sabina.* A Roman name. Fascinating. "Sabina," I say, resisting the urge to reach into her mind and wake her up. That would be hypocritical.

She lets out a tiny moan, and my cock jerks in response. It's been too long since I indulged my most primal urges, I tell myself. That's why she's having this effect on me. I like rescuing women but I don't usually want to fuck them—at least, not this badly or this soon.

"Sabina." I'm using a firmer tone of voice now. "Wake up." I'm impervious to the cold seeping through my suit pants as I kneel on the ground and cradle this half-naked woman, but I know the same can't be said for her. The ground is leeching away more of her body heat by the second.

When she still doesn't respond, I let out a huff of annoyance. "Fine. Have it your way."

I'm a big guy, but even if I weren't, I'd find her easy to lift. Being a vampire has some advantages. Scooping her up with one arm beneath her shoulders and the other beneath her knees, I stand and move over to the bench tucked in the corner of the private booth before sitting down and settling her in my lap. That's better.

She seems not to have registered that I've moved her. I let my gaze wander over her body, drinking in the slopes of her breasts, and the sharp way her torso dips in to a surprisingly slender waist which then curves out to broad, round hips. A diamond is winking in her belly button, and beneath the scrap of purple lace which people today seem to consider adequate underwear, I can make out the texture of her pubic hair. Her thighs are creamy, marred only by a tattoo of a lily on the left one.

Gods, I'm hard. And I can't sit here forever. For one thing, I'm on duty. And for another, if I wait much longer, the temptation will be too great and I'll do something self-indulgent, like reach between those creamy thighs and bring her back to consciousness by making her come harder than she ever has in her life.

The nipple Ethan pinched is a mite more swollen than the other and I have a sudden urge to taste it.

This has to stop.

"Sabina." I give her a little shake, wondering whether she's even aware that she has a Roman name. What the fuck did Ethan do to her just before he left? She was more conscious than this when I arrived on the scene.

In the end, I realize I have no choice. I reach briefly into her mind—hating myself for having to do so—and jolt her awake.

Her eyes snap open and she blinks several times before turning her dark blue gaze to me. Careful not to look directly into her huge pupils, I whisper gently, "You're all right. You're safe."

"What happened?" She bucks suddenly, trying to jerk herself out of my arms but I hold her easily.

"Hush, little one. It's all right. You're in Club Toxic. You were attacked but you're safe now. I'm a bouncer here."

"What?" She's still blinking, then glances down at herself and I can all but hear the blood rushing to her pretty face when she realizes she's missing her dress. "Let me go, you pervert!"

"Hey!" I say in a no-nonsense tone. "There's no need for that. I'll let you go in a moment but first I need to make sure you're all right."

She gives a little snort. "Sure. I'm fine. I'm lying practically naked in a complete stranger's arms in what looks very much like a changing room, but other than that..."

I bite back a grin. She has spirit. I like that. Still cradling her with one arm, I shrug awkwardly out of my suit jacket.

"You don't have to do that," she says, once again struggling to get up.

"Yes, I do."

"You don't! Just let me up and I'll put my dress back on." She follows my pointed gaze to where her outfit lies shredded on the floor. "Oh."

"You don't remember that happening?" I cover her with my jacket, a pang of regret shooting through me at the thought I'll never see those pert, pink little nipples again. What's wrong with me? I see tits all the time. And hers are cute, but they're not *that* special.

"I don't," she says softly. "Thank you for this." Drawing the jacket up to her pointy chin, she tries to meet my gaze and I make sure to look at the spot between her brows instead of directly into her eyes. Otherwise, I might be tempted to compel her to throw the jacket back off, spread those creamy thighs wide open for me, and—

"You're welcome. What's the last thing you remember?"

A little crease forms in her forehead as she thinks. "Going down a very long staircase. A shadowy man."

Her face is so expressive, I can all but see the thoughts as they form in her mind.

"There *is* a BDSM club down here! And he... Ethan... he wanted to play but we didn't talk first, didn't negotiate, nothing." She glances around the booth, almost as if she expects to see him standing in a corner. "Where is he, anyway?"

"He won't bother you again." He won't bother anyone again ever, if I have anything to do with it, but there's no need to frighten her. She's obviously confused enough.

"What's your name?"

The question takes me by surprise. Instead of focusing all her attention on her current predicament, she's asking about me. "Maximus," I say.

The corners of her full, pink lips quirk up. "Like a gladiator?"

I was a centurion, actually, but I merely nod. This isn't the first time I've had this conversation. "Something like that."

"I like it. I suppose everyone calls you Max, for short."

Unable to stop myself, I lower my voice, using the tone I reserve for wayward little sweetbloods. "Only once. Nobody ever dares to do it a second time."

A tiny shiver runs through her, and I'm surprised by how strongly she affects me. Then she visibly pulls herself together. "Well, Maximus, thanks very much for coming to my aid but I think I'd better be heading off home now. If you would kindly let me up..."

"You may get up but you're not going anywhere just yet," I say firmly. "You've been through a bit of an ordeal."

"All the more reason to head home and get into my jammies," she says, taking advantage of my brief inattention and slithering out of my arms before I can stop her. "A mug of hot chocolate and a good book, and I'll be fine."

"Did you drive yourself here?" I watch, faintly amused, as she stands before me, wobbling slightly in those ridiculous shoes, clutching my suit jacket uncertainly to her chest.

"I did. So?"

"How does your head feel?" I counter, wondering why she's being so damn stubborn.

She blinks, and the hand not holding my coat comes up to touch her forehead. "A bit woozy. Must have been the wine. You're right, I should probably wait a bit. I don't suppose you guys serve coffee here?"

"I'm sure I can organize some for you." Not many of the patrons ask for coffee but some of the human staff members insist on having it available. I've acquired a bit of a taste for it, myself.

"That would be great. Thank you. Um. I don't suppose I could borrow this for a while?" At my raised eyebrow, she indicates my suit jacket. "I'll bring it back tomorrow."

I rub my own forehead, wondering why she's getting to me so much. "Sure."

She hesitates for a second, obviously trying to decide whether or not to turn around. I bite back another grin. "I've already seen it all, sweetheart," I say.

The flush staining her cheeks is delicious. "Oh," she says in a small voice, whipping the jacket over her shoulders and shrugging her arms into the sleeves as fast as she can.

"Don't be ashamed. You have a stunning body."

Her blush deepens and I realize that, for the first time in a long time, I'm craving a specific person's blood. Hers.

"Thank you," she whispers, pulling the grey coat tightly around herself. Even though she's quite tall, it comes to mid-thigh, and the sleeves almost cover her hands completely. She looks like a child playing dress-up. "I'm Sabina, by the way."

"A Roman name," I say. "Did you know that?"

"I didn't! What a coincidence!" She bends to pick up the remains of her tattered dress—giving me a tantalizing glimpse of full, creamy white buttocks—and frowns. "I guess I can toss this."

"I'm sorry about Ethan," I say. "But if you barely knew him, what on earth possessed you to come down here with him?" I'm interested to hear what she says. While I don't doubt that he lured her down by using his compelling ability, I wonder how much she remembers, and whether she'll admit to anything else. She doesn't disappoint me.

"Curiosity." She shrugs and then gazes down at her feet. "I heard there was a BDSM club down here. I wanted to see whether the rumors were true. And he seemed all right. A bit stiff."

I let out a bark of laughter. "That's one way of putting it. Come on then, sweetheart, let's go to the bar and I'll see about getting you some coffee." Worried that she's still unsteady, I reach out to take her hand but she yanks it away.

"It's fine," she says. "I'll follow you."

Infuriating is the first word which comes to mind but I suppress a sigh. "If you don't want me to touch you, I won't, but I'm not letting you out of my sight. So you lead the way and I'll be right behind you."

"I'm a grown woman!" Her eyes flash with something akin to annoyance. She's certainly woken up from the groggy state she was in just a short while ago.

Refusing to rise to her bait, I lift an eyebrow and direct a pointed glance at her chest. "I had noticed."

Her huff as she turns and shoves back the curtain is nothing short of adorable. Ignoring her reaction, I simply follow her as she wobble-stalks toward the bar.

Sabina. I turn the name over in my mind, savoring it. And there was me thinking this would be yet another boring evening...

3

S *abina*

IF THERE'S one thing I cannot stand, it's being made to feel helpless. Vulnerable. Unable to look after myself. And if there's one thing the incredibly attractive man behind me is doing, it's making me feel just that. It's infuriating.

If it were up to me, I'd slink back up the stairs, sneak past the partygoers, and head straight to my car. Sure, I had a glass of wine, but that was quite some time ago now and I feel fine. Well... not fine, exactly, but definitely not inebriated.

What the hell did that Ethan guy do to me, anyway?

But this Maximus is as stubborn as a dog with a bone, and there's no way I'll be going anywhere while he's watching me. Moreover, I feel kind of safe with him, so what harm will it do to stay just a little longer? After all, I was passed out in his lap, practically naked, and he didn't take advantage, and I could really use a cup of coffee. My head feels so weird. Kind of buzzy but quiet at the same time. And there's a definite gap in my memory. I remember flashes of coming down here with Ethan, but they're more like slides in a reel than a cohesive movie.

We reach the bar and I sink gratefully onto a nearby stool. My feet are killing me, and I vow never to wear these stupid heels again. A pretty Goth bartender casts a skeptical eye over my outfit and I only just refrain from rolling my eyes. After all, this is a kink club. There are people who are literally naked performing the most explicit sex acts just feet away. Maximus leans over my shoulder and I catch a whiff of expensive aftershave. The man smells almost as good as he looks. Damn him. I do not need to be rescued.

"Two coffees, Alaya. Thanks, hon," he murmurs to the girl.

"Sure thing." She smiles sweetly at him and bustles off.

"Now, you turn to face me." Oh god. He's using that tone of voice again. That low, dominant tone which makes my knees turn to water and my heart skip a beat. He's usually more soft-spoken, which only highlights the difference. "Atta girl."

I let him swivel the stool around until I have my back to the rest of the club and all my attention is focused on him. He's tall—well over six feet—and has the broad shoulders you'd expect in a bouncer. Now that I'm wearing his suit jacket, he's left in a white shirt and a grey silk tie. It seems like very formal attire for a kink club but I remember the doormen outside also wearing suits. Maybe it's a uniform of sorts. It's a shame this evening deteriorated so fast and so badly. I really had been hoping for a good play session.

For some reason, the only time my chattering brain goes

quiet is when I lose myself in the sensations of pain and pleasure a good dominant can provide.

"How are you feeling now?" he asks, his gaze fixed on my face. I feel strangely exposed and vulnerable under his assessing attention. I don't like it.

"Like I already said, I'm fine," I tell him. It comes out more sharply than I had intended and I don't miss the flicker of aggravation as it crosses his handsome features.

"Your coffees, Maximus," the girl behind the bar says, setting two mugs down and bustling away. I hadn't realized we were right in the corner with even the closest people out of earshot.

"Thanks," he tells her, then returns his attention to me. His blue eyes are steely. "You should watch your tone," he says in a growl. "If I hadn't heard your cries for help and come to your rescue, right now you'd be—"

He stops speaking abruptly and I get the distinct feeling he'd been about to say something he shouldn't.

"I'd be... what?" I press, genuinely curious now.

"Never mind." Rubbing an impatient hand over his closely cropped dark hair, he reaches behind himself, takes one of the mugs and hands it to me. "Drink up."

There's something very strange about this whole situation. As the fogginess in my mind clears, I begin to feel more and more that this isn't a typical BDSM club. There's an underlying sense of danger I hadn't noticed before. It's in the air, and in the eyes of some of the people I passed. Overcome with curiosity, I swivel around on my stool and take a good look at my surroundings for the first time since entering the club.

"Nuh-uh," Maximus says, swiftly turning me back around so all I can see is him and the wall beyond. I bite down a surge of anger. Just who does he think he is?

"What?" I say belligerently. "I'm not allowed to look around now? What exactly is this place, anyway? What were you going to say about Ethan before? Why does it feel like I can't remember half of what happened since I got here? And who made you my keeper?" Once the questions start pouring out of me, I can't stop them, even as Maximus's gaze grows grimmer and his eyebrows rise higher and higher on his forehead.

"Are you quite finished?" he says, once I run out of breath.

"Are you going to give me any answers?" I counter.

"Sure. Of course you're allowed to look around but right now, we're having a conversation and I'd rather talk to your front than to your back. This place is, as you correctly surmised, a BDSM club. The owner likes to keep it secret as we only cater to exclusive clientele."

"Like Ethan?" I say drily, unable to stop myself.

Maximus pretends not to have heard me but I didn't miss the tic in his jaw when I said that. He presses on. "I can't say for sure what would have happened if I hadn't come to your aid earlier, but I'm sure you can come up with a few scenarios yourself. What do predators typically do when they have a beautiful woman ensnared? As for your trouble remembering, it wouldn't surprise me if he slipped something into your drink. Did he have any chance to do anything like that?"

I feel my face grow hot as I remember Ethan getting us the glasses of wine at the bar upstairs. I was so excited to finally get in that I made a dumb mistake. For god's sake, I'm thirty-five, not some college kid at her first bar. "He may have," I admit in a small voice, staring at my thighs so as not to see the reproach in Maximus's eyes.

"And no, I'm not your keeper," he continues. "But

looking after our guests is my job and I happen to take it seriously. So until I know you're fit to drive home, I will be keeping an eye on you."

"What if someone else needs your help in the meantime?"

"I'm not the only DM here. And I can see past you." The corner of his wide, generous mouth curls up, revealing a devastating dimple in his cheek. "I'm fairly good at multi-tasking, as every good dom should be."

Goddamnit, he has an answer for everything. I take a sip of coffee to hide how flustered I am as a sudden image enters my mind of me tied up, naked, writhing, dancing to his tune as he slaps me with one big hand and strokes my clit with the other.

"Want me to prove it?"

His growled question drags me out of my reverie and I'm not sure I heard correctly. "What?" I suddenly have difficulty looking at him.

"You heard me. Don't pretend the thought of me taking you somewhere private and making you walk that razor's edge of pleasure and pain doesn't make that secret place between your legs tingle."

I'm so stunned that all I can do is blink as a jolt of desire thumps through my core. I swallow past my suddenly dry throat and pretend to be unaffected. "I thought you were on duty?"

Once again he graces me with that lazy, lopsided smile so at odds with his firm stance and masculine presence. "I'm due a break soon."

"How long is your break?" I whisper, squeezing my thighs together against the sudden surge of longing between them.

"Long enough. So... how about it? Fancy a little playtime?" His expression is intense and it's then that I realize: this is a trick. He's testing me.

"What, and make the same mistake twice in one evening?" I'm livid at the idea that I almost fell for it. How desperate, how starved of pleasure must I be to even consider going back into one of those booths with yet another virtual stranger? "I don't think so." Shoving my mug into his hands, I slip off the stool. "I'm perfectly capable of driving now, so I think I'll head on home. Thanks for the coffee." I've just turned away when I feel him grip my shoulder.

"Wait," he says.

I spin back around, my heart pounding. "I appreciate your rescuing me, and it was lovely to meet you, Maximus. Thank you for lending me your jacket and I meant what I said, I'll bring it back tomorrow. Will this place be open?" I gabble, feeling more foolish by the second.

"It will." His composure only serves to heighten my anxiousness. "But haven't you forgotten something?"

That question catches me off-guard. "I can't think what."

He rakes me up and down with a look which makes me tingle all over. "Where are your keys?"

Shit. I cast my mind back over the events of the evening, trying to remember where I last had my purse. "In my bag."

"Which would be where?"

I don't know! I want to scream at him. "I don't suppose you saw it in the booth?"

"I didn't."

It's all getting to be too much. Hot tears sting my eyes but I blink them back, determined not to show weakness. "It may still be there. Or is there a lost and found here somewhere?"

"There is. Come on, let's go and look."

I've been strong and independent my entire life. I take care of others, it's what I do. I don't have people take care of me, and I certainly don't need a rescuer. If Maximus finds my purse before I do, he'll have rescued me twice in one evening. I can't bear the thought.

Still, my keys are in there, as well as my wallet and ID. My phone. I need that damn bag back. "Do you think Ethan took it?" I bleat, following Maximus as he threads his way back through the crowd on the dancefloor toward the private booths.

"No. Ethan's a slimy prick but he's not a thief."

"Is that how you refer to all your elite clientele?" I say cuttingly, but again, Maximus ignores my remark. Is he hard of hearing, or impervious to wit?

"We'll check here first, then we'll head to the office if necessary," he says, yanking the curtain aside. "Someone will have handed it in."

I take a deep breath before heading back into the booth where this whole nightmare began, wondering whether this interminable evening will ever end.

Fuck Zeke. Fuck Ethan. Fuck it all. I should never have come here.

4

M aximus

I HAVE no idea what possessed me to ask a girl in my care to play with me. Flirting is like second nature to me, and I have no shortage of sweetbloods to torment and tantalize, so it's not like I'm starved in any sense of the word. But there's just something about Sabina which sets her apart from other women, something that drives me crazy. In fact, I haven't felt this way since Caroline first barreled into my life.

Now there's a terrifying thought.

After what happened to her, I swore never, ever to feel that way about any woman again. Ever. So maybe it's not a bad thing that Sabina is so desperate to leave. Once we find her purse, that is.

I'm so caught up in my own thoughts that it takes me a moment to realize that Sabina is standing stock still, her lips slightly parted, her big, dark blue eyes round with shocked surprise. Glancing past her into the booth we've just entered, I see why.

It's occupied.

Quick as a flash, I take in the entire scene: Nina, an established club regular, is grinding back up against Bentley, a vampire who stops by here whenever he's in Tucson. Her skirt is hiked up around her waist and her eyes are closed, her head lolling back against his shoulder in ecstasy. Her bare breasts sport fresh welts—from a cane, perhaps, or maybe a crop—and Bentley's skilled fingers are working frantically between her slightly spread thighs as she writhes and moans.

"Please, Sir," she whimpers, reaching up to clutch at his head.

"Don't touch me," he barks, his fingers working faster as her hand falls back down to dangle limply at her side. "You know when—and not a second before."

A ragged breath is her only response. With the hand not rubbing her pussy, Bentley winds a chunk of her dark hair around his fist and yanks her head back to expose her throat. I know exactly what's going to happen next. I've seen it thousands of times. I've *done* it thousands of times. What's imperative is that Sabina doesn't see it.

A quick glance around is my saving grace. A rectangular, brightly beaded purse is tucked away in a dark corner.

"Sabina," I whisper, praying that she will hear me but the others won't. She turns to look at me and the naked, unashamed lust in her dark eyes jolts through my groin. "Leave quietly. I'll be right out. We don't want to disturb them."

She hesitates, and I hope against hope that I'm not forced to reach inside her mind to nudge her once more. *Just do it*, I think. As loath as I am to compel her, no matter how good the reason, doing that is still better than having to wipe her mind. And far less risky. The musky-sweet smell of feminine arousal permeates my nostrils and I wonder whether it's Nina or Sabina. Maybe both. I force the thought away.

"All right," she breathes, and I thank the gods when she turns back towards the curtain and slips out.

Either Bentley and Nina haven't yet noticed our intrusion or they simply don't care, caught up as they are in the throes of raw, primal lust. I slink into the corner and retrieve the purse just as Nina cries out. She's coming and Bentley is feeding, his fangs penetrating the soft skin of her throat as she humps his hand, her thighs trembling with the force of her climax.

Fuck, the mere sight is making me hungry. I wonder what Sabina tastes like. How she sounds when she's on the brink. Does she whimper, or scream? Some women come silently, holding their breath, the only proof of their orgasm being the way they contract around your fingers or shaft. Others grunt like feral beasts. My cock is rigid, straining in my pants and I reach down to adjust it. As soon as Sabina's out of here and I've finished my shift, I'll have to find a pretty little regular sweetblood to screw. Shannon, perhaps, or Tania. Drinking blood from the tap tonight simply isn't going to cut it. I need to lose myself in an armful of soft, female flesh. Drive this sudden uncontrollable lust out of my system.

I slip out of the booth with Nina's cries still echoing around it. Sabina is standing just outside, her eyes like saucers, clutching my jacket around herself like a shield. Then she clocks what I'm holding.

"Oh thank god," she says, rushing up to me and damn near yanking her purse out of my hands.

"You're welcome," I say, resisting the urge to roll my eyes.

But she's not listening. She's taken the phone out of her bag and is staring at the screen. Even in the dim, red glow of the club I can see the blood drain from her face. As flustered and turned on as she was moments ago, now she's just one thing: terrified.

"Is something wrong?"

"Huh?" Dragging her eyes up to my face, she gives me the most fake smile I've seen in a century. "No, nothing. It's fine." Her gaze flits back down to the screen, then she clicks off the phone and stuffs it back into her purse. "Everything's still here, thank goodness. Thank you for retrieving it for me."

"You're welcome." *It's not your business*, I tell myself firmly. *She's nobody to you.* Actually, that's not entirely true. She's fast becoming somebody to me, and it's for that exact reason that I need her to leave before my protective instinct ratchets any higher. "Are you sure you're all right?" my voice says anyway. I just can't fucking help myself.

"It's... I'm fine. My ex sent me a text, that's all. He's just mad because we broke up recently."

Leave it alone. No more questions. Escort her to the door and say goodbye. "Why did you break up?" *Damn it.*

Her big eyes narrow as she stares at me. "You're very inquisitive."

"You're right, I'm sorry. It's none of my business." I stuff my hands into my suit pants, almost chewing off my own tongue to stop myself from interrogating her further. Who's her ex? How recently did they break up? Why did they break up? What did the text message say, exactly? "Were you together long?"

She lets out a giggle, and I realize I said the last one out loud. Fuck. But then she responds. "Just a month. Not long at all."

"Well, I'm sorry." It's half a lie. I'm not sorry at all that they broke up if he's enough of a dick to be sending her nasty text messages. But losing someone can hurt, even if you know you're better off without them. I've been around long enough to know that.

"Like I said, it's fine." She slips the strap of her purse over her shoulder and flicks her hair back in a signal meant to demonstrate how together she is. Even though she can't fool me for a second, I play along.

"Ready to go?" I ask her and she nods. "Come on then."

We wind our way through the writhing bodies on the dancefloor, up the staircase, and out through the coat check booth. The bar upstairs has emptied out considerably compared to earlier; it must be getting late. I'm walking behind Sabina, wondering whether she's aware that people turn to look at her when she goes past them. She must be. Still, if that's the case, she's remarkably unaffected by it. Most attractive women are aware of their effect on people. And if there's one thing I cannot stand, it's arrogance.

Once we reach the doors leading outside, she comes to such an abrupt stop that I almost bump into her. "Well, Maximus," she says softly, holding out a hand for me to shake. "It was nice meeting you. Will you be here tomorrow so I can return your coat?"

I take her hand and squeeze it a mite harder than I probably should. She winces and, once again, a jolt of lust shoots through my gut. I want to make her wince more. I want to take her back down into the club, chain her to the wall, or perhaps tie her over a spanking bench, and push her to the brink of agony over and over again until her inner thighs are slick and she's begging for my cock. My teeth. I press the tip of my tongue against my incisor, feeling the sharp point. "Are you sure you don't need me to walk you to your car? Where are you parked?"

"Just around the corner. Don't worry. I'm a big girl and I can take care of myself. And your duty of care to me ends here, doesn't it?" she says with a sweet, slightly ironic smile.

In more ways than one. "I'll be here tomorrow," I say. I don't care about the damn jacket and normally I'd tell her to keep it. In fact, I should, but for some reason, I really want to see her again tomorrow, even if it's just for a minute.

What is wrong with me?

"Good. I'll return this then." Giving a little shiver, she extracts her hand from mine and wraps the coat tighter around herself. "It's certainly cooled down since earlier."

I just nod, suddenly desperate for her to go before I give in to any of the temptations which have been haunting me for the past hour or so.

"Drive safely," I say. "And... hey. Don't let your dumb ex get you down. He's probably just being a dick because his feelings are hurt."

A flicker of something crosses her expression but then again she visibly pulls herself together. "Thanks. And you're probably right. He probably didn't mean it."

I watch her clack off down the street in those heels she obviously rarely wears, wondering what that last statement was all about. Mean what? Did he threaten her? The sudden protective rage which surges up in my chest at the thought takes me by surprise.

I glance at the sky, calculating how long I have left before I need to be home. Wondering where Sabina lives. The temptation to get into my own car and follow her is strong, but it's too risky for several reasons. Number one, I'm still on duty and to a casual observer, I've spent far too much time with just one club guest as it is. Number two, I would be forced to lurk around outside her place unless or until she noticed me hovering and invited me in. Which would lead to number three—I would come off as creepier than fucking Ethan if she caught me loitering outside her home. And number four: no place to hide when the sun makes its inevitable appearance in just a few short hours' time. I can't know how Sabina lives—house or apartment, basement or high up. But I can pretty much guarantee there'd be nowhere for me to safely spend the daylight hours.

Being a vampire is such a fucking drag sometimes.

Sabina's shapely form disappears around the corner and I congratulate myself on my restraint as I head back into the club. I used to be such a hot-head, but I've mellowed over the last few centuries.

At least, I like to think so...

5

S *abina*

FUCKING, fucking Zeke. How very dare he? Tossing the ridiculous shoes into the backseat of my car, vowing once more never to wear them again, I turn on the ignition and set off on the—thankfully, fairly short—journey home, my thoughts tumbling over each other, wondering abstractedly whether this is what it feels like to be on speed.

His text message was short and to the point: *I warned you never to go to Club Toxic.*

What the hell is that even supposed to mean? I take a corner too fast and force myself to breathe deeply, to try and regain some control—at least until I get home. Is it meant to be a threat? A genuine warning? Or is he just trying to mess with me? How the fuck does he know where I was? Is he watching me, or having me watched? Did someone else spy on me for him?

My knuckles are white as I clutch the steering wheel of my ancient Explorer, my whole body trembling.

First that Ethan guy, and now this. It's like the universe is conspiring against me. And the one nice thing to come out of it—meeting that devastatingly attractive Maximus—now feels tainted, somehow. Not to mention, I shouldn't read too much into his apparent concern. As bouncer/dungeon monitor/whatever his job title, he gets paid to look after guests. Sure, he offered to walk me to my car, but even so. And yes, he asked me to play with him, but I'm ninety-nine percent sure that was a test to see whether I'd be dumb enough to enter a private booth with a virtual stranger twice in one evening.

I'm not that stupid, regardless of how handsome he is, or how that dominant tone in his voice makes me squirm in a good way.

Just the memory of his invitation makes my core clench, and I let out a frustrated groan, slamming the palm of my hand against the steering wheel as I wait at a red light.

A man that devastating probably already has a girl-friend or wife, and if he doesn't, he's likely a shameless flirt. And I've had enough of men like that, thank you very much.

Still, though. I bet he'd be fun to play with. The trouble with womanizers is often that they're so very, very good at the art of seduction—and following through. Experience is the best teacher.

I'm still kicking myself inwardly for letting the entire evening spiral so madly out of control when I pull into the little parking spot I rent along with my condo. It's not until I'm about to get out of the car that I remember I'm only wearing Maximus's suit jacket and my panties. Luckily, it's so early in the morning, the chances of there being anybody to witness my walk of shame are low. Even on a Friday night, most sensible people are in bed right now.

Usually, I'm one of them.

I unlock the iron gate, lock it again behind me, and hurry up the little path to my front door, wincing as I catch a small pebble with my bare foot. The complex I live in is expensive but fairly secure, something I'm glad of as I let myself in and drop my clutch on the coffee table. Even though I'm beyond tired, I desperately want a shower before going to bed. I need to wash every last trace of that creepy Ethan from my body.

So much for a wild night of play.

My condo is on two levels but the master bedroom and bath are on the first so I don't have to climb any steps as I head to my bedroom. Felix is lying on my bed, a disdainful look on his fluffy face. "Hey, sweetie," I tell him, dropping a kiss between his little ears. "Did you miss me?"

He hops off the bed and slinks away in response, and I suppress a chuckle. Usually I'm a dog person but this condo is too small. Nor would I want to leave a dog home alone all day while I'm at work. So I wound up getting a cat from the local shelter. One look at his golden eyes and I was a goner. "I'll take that as a yes," I tell him anyway, and shrug out of Maximus's jacket before laying it carefully over a chair.

The shower is as soothing as I had hoped and I stand in the spray for a long time, wishing I could just shut my mind off as easily as a faucet can be twisted. I've tried so many things... meditation, therapy, medication... nothing quiets and calms me the way pain does. I guess I'm just wired differently, although it took me a long time to accept that.

Zeke didn't get it, which is one reason why I broke it off with him. The main reason, though, was his weird attitude and volatile temper.

I had enough histrionics growing up, thank you very much. Now I'm in my mid-thirties, I try to maintain as much calm in my life as I can.

Rinsing the last of the conditioner from my hair, I breathe in the sweet-smelling steam and try in vain to stop the image of Maximus's handsome face from once again appearing in my mind. It's almost like he brainwashed me— I can't stop thinking about him. He's calm, almost too calm, with his soft-spoken voice and pale blue eyes. But there's something simmering beneath that cool exterior; a sense of white hot passion. And a worldliness I can't really describe.

Not many men I've met have a natural, easy dominance, but he definitely does. The way he took charge the minute he came to rescue me. The way he wouldn't let me leave right away. It could have come across as creepy but instead I felt weirdly safe, despite what had happened.

God, I'm still not entirely sure what exactly happened. I've been blind drunk before, but I've never felt like I did when I woke up in Maximus's lap. Ethan must have spiked my wine; there's no other explanation for the fogginess, the inability to remember details.

Bastard.

I wonder what would have happened if I'd met Maximus first. If his invitation to play had been genuine. Just the memory of the way his soft voice suddenly changes to a growl makes my tummy clench. I can almost hear him now, keeping me on the edge, that low tone in my ear telling me, "Not yet, don't you come yet…"

It's no good, I realize as I dry myself off and slip naked between the sheets. I'll never be able to sleep unless I do something about the pounding desire between my thighs.

My clit is already rigid before I begin to stroke it softly, my eyes closed, picturing that attractive couple in the booth.

The way the welts on the girl's breasts stood out stark red against her pale flesh. The way the man's fingers were working between her thighs. She was trembling with lust—I could so easily put myself in her place—leaning back against a strong, commanding man as he brings me ruthlessly, relentlessly to the very edge of pleasure, my slick pussy coating his hand as he rubs... rubs...

My own thighs are trembling as I imagine it's Maximus behind me, his breath warm on my neck, his heady scent surrounding me as he drives me closer and closer to orgasm. My fingers have become his fingers sliding up and down on my swollen clit as he growls in my ear, "Don't you dare... not yet... not until I say... don't you fucking *dare* come—"

My climax is long and hard, my whole body shaking with the force of it, my moans muffled by my tightly compressed lips. My sex floods and clenches, feeling suddenly, achingly empty.

"Wow," I murmur at length, pushing my hair out of my face and letting out a ragged breath. It's been a while since I came that hard. It's just as well Maximus can't read people's minds—he'd have a field day if he knew the effect he has on me.

As I drift off to sleep, my last thought is of him. I already know I have to see him again.

~

Maximus

SUNRISE IS CREEPING EVER CLOSER, and I can't help but feel relieved as Club Toxic slowly but surely empties out. I'm exhausted, even though there's no real reason to be. It was a fairly standard night—aside from the fact that I met the most fascinating female I've come across in a long time.

The odd thing is that I can't even say why I find her so interesting. But tall, blonde, stubborn Sabina has been in my thoughts ever since she hurried away in my suit coat and very little else.

Maybe it's because she turned down my offer to play. Women don't usually turn me down. That probably sounds arrogant—who knows, maybe it is—but it's a fact. Working security at a club is definitely a great way to meet ladies. *Or gentlemen, if you're so inclined*, I think, nodding to Tiberius as he strides past.

I'm sitting on the stool Sabina sat on earlier, sipping my glass of ethically-sourced blood, asking myself why the fuck I'm not balls-deep in a willing female right now.

When she left, I had every intention of seducing an easy sweetblood, of losing myself in a pretty girl's seductive scent and soft skin. But as I looked around, for some reason all I could see was Sabina's face. Not one of the numerous women still milling around the club—both upstairs and down—managed to raise so much as a flicker of interest.

Wonderful.

For the millionth time, I wonder what was in that text message she received. What made her smooth forehead crinkle with concern, what made worry flash in her big blue eyes. Fucking technology. We managed without all that shit for hundreds—thousands—of years. Now people are glued to their screens, accessible within seconds no matter how far apart in the world they are. It's not healthy, and I dread to think where it will all lead.

Still, if I had her number, I can't say with absolute certainty that I wouldn't do the same thing: send her a message to find out whether she got home safely. Which is another strange thought. Usually, once a guest leaves the club, it's out of sight, out of mind.

As much as part of me hopes she'll return tomorrow—tonight, technically—another part of me is praying she won't. Something tells me I wouldn't let her go again so easily, and that would go against my strict nothing-deep policy. I have too many people to take care of. I can't afford to focus on just one person.

If anything, this evening was the perfect proof of that. What if someone else had got themselves into trouble? What if someone did, and I don't know about it because I spent all fucking night either with or thinking about the blonde with the Roman name?

Ethan isn't the only predator around. I wasn't lying, we do have a strict policy with regards to vampires who attend the club, but you don't get to be centuries old without learning a thing or two about manipulation. We have a good team here at Toxic, we weed out the nasties fairly swiftly, but there are always new ones to take their place.

"Maximus." Alaya's soft voice cuts into my thoughts. I turn to see her wiping down the bar. "I'm about ready to head off, is there anything else you need before I go?"

"No. Thanks." Draining my glass, I set it down for her to take, suppressing a shudder at the stale taste of old, chilled blood. Yes, it's better than the old way; yes, it's more civilized, and I guess many of us have got used to the taste. But I will always prefer it hot and fresh, straight from the source. Fun fact: vampires can taste the chemicals in a person's blood, and fear and pain make it sweeter. As does arousal—to me, anyway.

And yet again, I'm wondering what Sabina tastes like. If this continues for much longer, I'll have to perform a mind wipe on myself. I suppress a grin at the thought.

A quick glance at my pocket watch confirms what years of instinct is already telling me: it's time to head off if I want to be safely home before the sun rises.

"Jesus, Maximus, why don't you come into the twenty-first century and get yourself a newer watch?" Liam asks me as I slide off the stool and slip the timepiece back into my pocket. "That thing's ancient! A relic."

"That's why I like it," I say. "They don't make quality like that these days." It was brand new when I received it; glistening gold. Flawless. A gift from Caroline on our first anniversary. She'd saved and saved to get it for me, putting aside every extra penny she earned making accessories for hats. She had nimble fingers and a good eye, and specialized in silk flowers. People came from all over, wanting her personally to create unique pieces to adorn their outfits. I told her she didn't need to work, but she was stubborn like that. She was good at it, and she loved it. Who was I to deny her something she loved?

Women don't wear hats anymore. Or corsets, or girdles, or garters. No, they wear men's jackets and ridiculous shoes.

I run a hand back and forth over my head—a bad habit of mine—as I finish saying my goodbyes, emerge into the night, and make for my car. It's time to go home, to hole up in my basement boudoir and await the setting of the sun.

Hopefully, a solid day's sleep will erase a certain blonde from my mind.

Somehow, deep down, I don't believe it will.

And that's unfortunate.

6

S *abina*

I DON'T KNOW why I'm so nervous but I can't help it. I've been jittery all day, and Zeke's stupid text messages are probably the main cause—although some of it might also be due to the fact that I'll be seeing Maximus again.

I woke up to yet another message from Zeke: *We need to talk.*

Of course I ignored it. Either he wants to get back with me, in which case he'd be wasting his breath, or he wants to give me a piece of his mind, in which case he can go to hell. Either way, not for a single second did I entertain the idea of replying.

A few hours later, my phone vibrated again. *You can't ignore me forever. Don't make this harder than it has to be.*

For the life of me, I cannot figure out what his deal is. What exactly is he trying to accomplish with these texts?

True, we only dated for a short time, but four weeks is long enough to figure someone out, and if he paid any attention to me at all, he'd know that I'm not the kind of girl to be bullied. Not by anyone. I didn't go into specifics about my past—it's none of anybody's damn business, as far as I'm concerned—but I told him enough. That my father skipped out on us when I was five. That my mother sought refuge in a bottle shortly after that. That raising my two younger siblings somehow became my job from that point on.

When you have to grow up fast, you get tough. I didn't have a choice. And to this day, I have a real problem with people who think they can boss me around. Had Zeke just one ounce of sensitivity, he would have realized that. If he wanted me to agree to talk to him, he would merely have had to adopt a different tone. Instead, it's like he's rubbing me the wrong way on purpose, and it's enough to make a girl want to scream.

I'm in my car on my way to the club when my phone sounds off again. I switched Zeke's ringtone to the *Jaws* theme, and my fingers tighten on the steering wheel when I hear that ominous tone. Once I've parked, I take my cell out of my bag. *Stay away from Club Toxic, Sabina. Last warning.*

What the actual fuck? Is he watching me? I realize how little I really know about Zeke. He hangs out at some motorcycle club or something, but I only ever saw a couple of his friends, and he never took me there. He works as a mechanic, or so he says, and he tends to get aggressive when he's had a few beers. He wasn't particularly sensitive or loving towards me, and when I dumped him, he merely nodded and said, "Fine," so this sudden display of interest is taking me by surprise.

Not a little unsettled, I slip my phone back into my bag and clamber out of my car, reassuring myself as I shake back my hair and get Maximus's jacket off my backseat. Zeke always did like a good head-fuck, and that's probably all this is. Just immature posturing. Maybe he went to Toxic at some point and had a bad time. Maybe he knows someone who works there. Maybe he's just guessing correctly that the first thing I would do after we broke up was what he'd expressly forbidden me to do.

I'm sometimes contrary like that.

A tiny voice inside my head asks whether this might be his weird way of looking out for me, but I quash that thought quickly. Even Zeke, who has all the sensitivity of a doorknob, would word well-intended messages better. At least, I'd hope so.

Taking a deep breath, I lock my car and smooth down my dress. At first, I debated whether or not to wear another one of my special dresses after one of my favorites got ruined last night, but then I figured it was highly unlikely that the same thing would happen again. Besides, the thought of seeing Maximus again made me reach for this one automatically. It's a deep purple color, and clings to my body in all the right places. Even though it looks pretty demure from the front, it has a plunging back, so wearing a bra with it is out of the question. I added some black, strappy sandals—a little kitten heel, but nothing outrageous this time—and left my hair loose to complete the look. I can only hope Maximus likes it.

Although why I want to impress him, I still don't know.

The queue of people waiting to get into Club Toxic is already stupidly long again but I put on a confident expression, push my shoulders back, and walk straight to the front, thanking the heavens that the two guys at the door are the same ones who were here yesterday. I vaguely remember

Ethan referring to one of them as Liam, so I try that when they notice me.

"Hi, Liam," I say loudly, paying close attention to see which one reacts. The blond one. Right. "Maximus is expecting me."

My heart is pounding and I hold my breath, hoping against hope that Maximus is even in the club. To be sent away now would be both devastating and humiliating, considering dozens of people are watching me.

For once, I'm in luck.

"Go on in," Liam says, stepping aside.

Not until I've passed under the refreshing blast of air-conditioning do I allow myself to exhale. And it's then that I realize I never planned further ahead than this moment. In all likelihood, Maximus is downstairs. And I have no idea how to get down there without an express invitation. Seeing as the entrance is hidden in the coat check area, I highly doubt that just anyone is allowed to march on down the steps.

Crap.

There's a bored-looking guy sitting in the coat check booth, and I approach him with my most winning smile. "Hi," I say, glad I sound more confident than I feel. "I'm here to see Maximus."

"Is he expecting you?"

"Yep." It's only half a lie. I did tell him I'd return his coat today. But if I say that, this guy might take the jacket and promise to pass it on, and I can't bear the thought of having to leave again without seeing the man who's been on my mind for nearly twenty-four hours now. "He said I should just ask for him here and that you'd let me go down."

The guy's eyebrows rise and I suppress a groan. Maybe

that was too far-fetched? "He said that, did he?" The dude sounds skeptical.

"He did. If you don't believe me, call him up here. It's no difference to me." I shrug as casually as I'm able to.

"It's just—I can't let you go down there unescorted," the guy says. He has a narrow, attractive face, albeit a bit pale.

I lift my chin. "Can't *you* escort me then?"

The corner of his mouth lifts and he shakes his head. "Someone needs to man the booth."

"Then I'd say we have a bit of a dilemma, don't we?"

Another man in a dark suit arrives then, and the first guy visibly brightens. "Augustus. Would you please escort this young lady down to the club?"

What is with this place and Roman names, anyway? I wonder.

Augustus's eyebrows go up and he looks first at me, then back at the coat check guy. "Sure."

It's all I can do to suppress the grin of triumph from spreading over my face.

Result.

"Thank you," I say sweetly, entering the booth without an invitation and threading my arm through Augustus's.

"She's here to see Maximus," the first man says. It seems like Augustus is superior to him, and he feels the need to explain himself.

"It's fine," Augustus says. "I was about to head down anyway." He punches a code into a keypad beside the door —funny, I never noticed Ethan doing that yesterday—and it slides open to reveal the stairwell. "Have you known Maximus long?" he asks casually as we begin to descend the steps.

"Not very," I admit. Augustus is very attractive, I notice,

with his closely cropped beard and rugged features. He's not a patch on Maximus, though.

"I see."

I'm tempted to ask what exactly he means by that, but then we've reached the downstairs club, and my heart begins to pound in my chest at the thought of seeing Maximus again in just a few short moments. I can't believe I actually made it back in here on my own steam.

Augustus scans the area, and I don't miss the way his nostrils flare. If anything, the club is even more busy than it was yesterday, but there's just one face I'm looking for in the crowd.

"Over there, in the corner." Augustus points. "I assume you can make your way alone from here?" His accent is also strange, also slightly British. What exactly is it with these club employees?

"Of course. Thank you." Sure enough, there he is, barely discernible in the red gloom, but even after such a brief time, I'd recognize those broad shoulders anywhere.

"Have fun," Augustus says, and as I turn to cross the dancefloor, I half expect him to pat my butt. He doesn't.

This is it. Be cool, I tell myself as I take yet another deep breath and thread my way through the throng.

Maximus is watching someone else; he hasn't spotted me yet. Once I'm a few feet away, I will him to look at me and, as if by magic, he does. Our eyes meet, and a jolt of something I've never felt before slams through my system, making me blink.

Curiouser and curiouser.

"Sabina," he says, getting up off his stool and pressing a kiss to my cheek. His lips are strangely cool. "How did you get down here?"

"I brought back your jacket," I blurt out, suddenly

completely unnerved by his proximity. Then I kick myself for acting so stupidly. *For god's sake, you're a grown woman*, I scold myself. *Not a teenager with her first crush.*

"I see that." Am I imagining it, or is he bemused? "Thank you." I hand him the coat and he takes it, slinging it over the crook of his arm. Once again, he's wearing a suit. I wonder how many he owns. And that leads me to wondering what his closet looks like. His bedroom...

There's a long, awkward pause, during which I find myself wishing the ground would swallow me up. "Um. Are you on duty?" I say at length. Anything to break the silence.

"Not tonight, no."

For a second, I'm filled with a blind hope that he's only here because he knew I'd come. But that's a ridiculous notion. Nothing in his demeanor ever suggested he was more interested in me than any bouncer is in a club guest.

Although, he did ask you to play, a little voice says in the back of my mind.

"Well, since you came all this way, would you like a drink?" he asks at length.

"I'd love one. Thank you."

He gestures toward the bar and inclines his head in a strangely polite nod. The movement reminds me of the way men conduct themselves in Jane Austen movies. "After you," he says.

Giving him a shy smile, I turn and head towards the bar, hoping that my exposed back will have the intended effect on him. He's here. He's not on duty. He's asked me to have a drink with him.

Tonight is already shaping up to be way better than yesterday...

7

M*aximus*

EVEN THOUGH I had been hoping Sabina would show up again tonight, I hadn't realized just how strong that hope was until she was standing there before me, looking stunning in a purple, knee-length dress. *Breathtaking*, I think—not that I have any breath left to take. In fact, I only breathe around humans so as not to unsettle them.

When she turns around, my cock jerks at the expanse of smooth, white back she's displaying to me. The globes of her ass are accentuated by the clingy material, and suddenly my fingers are itching to touch her.

What the fuck is it with this girl? I'm reminded of the time when I was a young lad in Rome. Our neighbor had a beautiful wife who used to walk around their outside rooms naked, knowing full well anybody who went past could see her. Even though she seemed pretty old to me at the time—

comparatively, anyway, she may have been in her thirties—that woman fueled many of my adolescent fantasies. I damn near rubbed my cock raw thinking about the things I'd like to do to her... and have her do to me. It was so many hundreds of years ago now—gods, well over a millennia and a half—and I still remember how the mere sight of her made a bolt of lust punch through my gut.

Sabina is having the same effect on me now.

I notice her shoes. Still pretty, but much more sensible. The straps wind around her ankles and go up her calves. *Gladiator sandals*, I find myself thinking.

It's a good thing I'm off duty, as all I can focus on is the shapely woman walking in front of me, like a slavering dog with a bone. And it's then that I realize: this is lust. Not love. It's nothing like what I had with Caroline. How could it be, when I know next to nothing about Sabina? You can't love someone you don't even know.

The realization is comforting. Love, you cannot control. Lust is a whole different animal. Lust, you can slake. I can screw this woman into submission and out of my system, and then we can both go our separate ways. She won't even have to find out I'm a vampire.

Sabina reaches the bar and perches on the same stool in the corner I made her sit in last night. Her dress has ridden up her thighs, and I wonder idly whether she's wearing panties. She probably is, she did yesterday. Although I never did see the point in what they call G-strings—that tiny strip of satin or lace or whatever barely covers anything. Maybe they were designed with sadists in mind. I do like to yank them tight against a girl's pussy until she's afraid to move for fear of the pain. Then I realize Sabina is looking at me with a shy smile.

"Are we going to have that drink?" she says softly, and I curse inwardly that she caught my moment of inattention.

"What would you like?"

"A double gin and tonic?"

She's phrased it like a question. I grin at her. "Are you asking, or ordering?"

When she looks down, I notice how long her lashes are and wonder whether they're real.

"Ordering," she says.

I lift a hand to summon Alaya's attention. "One double gin and tonic, and one Scotch. You know how I like it," I tell her.

"Coming right up." The dark-haired bartender hurries away to get our drinks, and I resume my study of Sabina.

She's blatantly nervous, and I wonder why. It might just be excitement to be back here, to be seeing me again, but there's an undercurrent of tension that implies something more sinister. "Did you get everything sorted out?" I ask, fishing.

"Huh? Get what sorted out?"

I make myself comfortable on the stool beside hers and sling the jacket over my lap. All the better to hide my hard-on. "You seemed troubled when you left last night. That text you received?"

A myriad of emotions flicker over her face before she resumes her former cool expression. "It's nothing," she says casually. "Just my ex being a dickwad."

Oh, how I miss the days when ladies didn't swear. When showing a bare ankle was considered immodest. All right, I wouldn't go that far. "But he's not threatening you or anything? You're not in danger?"

"No," she snaps, a mite too quickly. Then, recovering

herself, "He's just a weirdo. I should never have gotten involved with him."

"What's his name?" My instincts are very rarely wrong, and I just know there's more to this. And even though one could argue it's none of my business, I can't help it. If anyone intends to hurt her, I want to know about it.

You *want to hurt her*, I think. *But only in delicious ways.*

"I don't want to talk about him," Sabina says, lifting her chin in a tiny gesture of defiance. "Thank you," she adds as Alaya sets a tall glass down on the bar beside my tumbler of whisky.

"Fair enough. Then we won't talk about him," I say. *Yet.* "What do you want to talk about?"

"I... I don't know." She takes a huge gulp of her drink, and I wonder again why she's so on edge.

"Was yesterday your first time here? I don't recall seeing you here before."

"It was."

"Then I'm even more sorry you had such a shitty time."

She looks up at me, then, and I'm struck by the look in her deep blue eyes. "Ethan was shitty," she says. "Meeting you... wasn't."

Ethan. I've been keeping an eye out, but that slimy bastard hasn't reappeared here so far. Just as well, since I haven't had a chance to talk to Lucius about him yet. "I'll take that as a compliment," I tell her.

She smiles shyly. "That's how it was intended." The pale column of her throat works as she swallows more of her drink, and it makes me want to lick my lips. My fangs will be buried in that milky skin before the night is done, I vow. I take a huge slug of whisky to distract myself.

There's a brief period of silence, which is strangely comfortable and charged with sexual tension at the same time. I do love this part—the flirting before the play. The play before the fuck. The fuck before the feed...

Sabina shifts on her stool, uncrossing and re-crossing her legs, and my acute sense of smell picks up the tiniest trace of her arousal, even despite the million other smells surrounding us.

Fuck, I want to bite her thighs.

"My invitation from yesterday still stands," I tell her in a low voice. "If you'd like to play, I'd be happy to oblige you."

She's wearing a delicate silver chain, and the crescent moon pendant nestled in the hollow of her throat is jumping in time with her pulse. I can almost feel her breath catch.

I so love a responsive woman.

"I..." She swallows again. Thinks for a moment. Then, in a decided voice, she says, "I'd like that. Sir."

She added the honorific as an afterthought but it has the intended effect. My cock twitches in my suit pants. "I assume you've some experience?" I say.

"I do. That's actually why I came here yesterday. It's been a while since I had a good scene."

"Your ex didn't satisfy you?"

"I told you, I don't want to talk about him," she snaps.

That's answer enough for me, but the game has begun and I need her to realize that. "Watch your tone, young lady," I growl at her, gratified by the instant change in her expression. "Uncross your legs."

Sabina hesitates for the briefest second before doing as she's told.

"Spread your thighs a little further apart." Another waft of her unique, sweet but musky scent hits my nostrils as she complies. I lay my palm on her knee, then slide my hand slowly up her left thigh, allowing my fingers to trace their way down and around until my knuckles are almost grazing her mound. Then I use one of my favorite tricks: capturing a tiny bit of sensitive skin between my nails and pinching her inner thigh cruelly, slowly increasing the pressure. "Look at me."

Her pupils are so huge, they've almost wiped out the blue of her irises. Her nipples are poking against the flimsy material of her dress. "Does that hurt?" I ask her.

She nods breathlessly, then lets out a gasp as I pinch harder.

"First rule if you're going to play with me: always be respectful. That includes no swearing. Do I make myself clear?"

She nods again.

"I can't hear you."

"Yes, Sir." She lets out a little gasp as I release the pressure.

"Good girl." Gods, I'm already so turned on, I have no idea how I'm going to pace myself. "Now, let's have a little talk about safewords and limits."

"Garlic," she says.

I fight to hide my amused surprise. "I beg your pardon?"

"My safeword is garlic." She shrugs. "Because I hate it."

It's a common misconception that vampires cannot stand garlic. I happen to love the stuff. Is this some kind of hint? A test? Surely it can't be sheer coincidence. However, my raging erection forces me to stay on course. "All right. Garlic it is. And limits?"

"I'm not a big fan of humiliation," she says quietly. "Verbal, at least. Being insulted, that kind of thing."

"Noted." The only usual way a submissive ends up having that sort of limit is when she's been abused in some way, and I bite back the fury I feel at whomever caused this stunning creature that kind of torment. "But you like pain?"

The blush staining her cheeks is visible even in the low light. "Very much."

"Shall we go see how much?" I'm trying not to get too excited. A lot of submissives overestimate what they can take. I've had girls beg me to hurt them, only to scream blue murder the moment I've delivered the first stroke. But she took that first excruciating little taste I gave her without making a sound, and I didn't miss the way her pulse quickened as my nails tightened in her sensitive flesh. Maybe I've struck gold.

"Yes please, Sir," she whispers. "May I please finish my drink and go visit the bathroom first?"

The difference between her over-confident, defensive side and this demure sweetness is like night and day. I just don't know which is the real her. "You may," I tell her. "Meet me back here."

After draining her gin and tonic, Sabina sets the glass down carefully on the bar and heads off in the direction of the restrooms. I watch her go, my cock pounding in my slacks. Her buttocks wobble as she walks, and I suppress a smile as I think of all the wicked things I'm going to do to her tonight.

I'm going to make Sabina scream...

8

S *abina*

IT'S ACTUALLY GOING to happen. I'm actually going to play with Maximus. I feel like I'm floating as I emerge from the bathroom and head back towards where he's waiting for me by the bar.

Usually one to linger in the ladies', I hurried this time, only casting a quick glance at my reflection as I washed my hands after. My eyes were blazing, my cheeks flushed. My nipples were clearly visible through my dress, as if they were already aching for his fingers.

He's so attractive, I find myself thinking as I reach him and he stands up, extending the arm not holding his jacket. I notice a strap slung over his shoulder: a toy bag. When did he get that? Where did he get it from? Maybe he keeps it behind the bar, just in case he comes across a little sub he wants to play with. Pushing that thought away, I slip my hand into the crook of his elbow, my heart hammering.

So what if he's not husband material? I don't need anyone, anyway. I'm not looking for a husband. I'm looking for a good time, and this gorgeous, tall, broad-shouldered hunk with strange, smoldering eyes is basically guaranteeing me one.

Yep, this is already shaping up to be a much better night than yesterday.

"I think booth one is free," he says in his soft, gruff voice. "Or would you like to go somewhere more public?" He inclines his head toward the open play stations lined up along the far wall.

"Private is fine," I say, glad he's given me the choice. I don't enjoy public play much. "I trust you."

The corner of his mouth quirks up and something flashes in his eyes. "First mistake," he says.

I raise an eyebrow questioningly but he doesn't elaborate. Instead he leads me over the dancefloor, through the throng of club goers, and whisks me into the private alcove.

Once inside, I glance around. It's not unlike the one I was in yesterday. A thick, heavy velvet curtain separates us from the rest of the club, muffling the sounds of music and voices. A shiny black St. Andrew's Cross is leaned up against one wall. There's a sex swing in the corner, and my knees almost give out at the image of myself lying in it, being rocked back and forth on Maximus's hard cock.

We haven't discussed that, I realize—whether sex is even on the menu. I wonder how to bring it up, how to let him know that I'd absolutely be down for it, and can't think of a way. Maybe it will happen organically. He's in charge right now, I remind myself. If he decides he wants to fuck me, I'm sure he'll make that known.

"Strip," he growls suddenly. That tone of voice makes all the hairs on the back of my neck stand on end and I hesitate for only a moment before tugging my dress over my head. He saw most of me naked yesterday, after all.

He's set his bag down in the corner and has shrugged out of his suit jacket, taken off his tie, and unbuttoned his shirt at the neck. If he rolls up his sleeves, I'll be a goner. Crouching down, he starts rummaging through his implements, and although I'm desperate to see what kinds of things he has in there, I focus instead on slipping my panties down my thighs. I'm wadding them into a little ball, not sure what to do with them, when I realize he's gazing at me, his expression intent. "Give those to me," he says.

I do, and he raises them to his nose, inhaling deeply, his nostrils flaring. A combination of shame and arousal makes my face prickle.

"Delicious," he says, putting them in his pocket. "I'll hang on to them for now."

I stand there awkwardly in the middle of the booth, not sure where to look or what to do with my hands. Crossing them in front of my chest would make me look defensive, so I simply put them behind my back, gripping one with the other.

Maximus rises from his crouched position and turns to face me, his eyes roving over my naked body. "Are your shoes comfortable?" he says.

"They're not hurting."

"Then keep them on." He takes a step toward me. It's not cold in the booth, but my nipples are still jutting out. I can feel my pulse beating between my legs. "Turn around. Slowly."

It's almost as if I can feel him appraising me but I do as

I'm told, rotating to give him a complete 360 view, hoping he likes what he sees.

"You're beautiful, Sabina," he says softly, and a rush of delight warms my chest.

"Thank you," I croak.

"Tiny waist. Makes me wonder what you'd look like in a corset." He begins to roll up his sleeves and I look away, desperate to retain some control over my arousal.

"Eyes on me," he growls, and I comply.

What choice do I have?

"Ever worn a corset?" he says.

I shake my head. "No, Sir." I'm hoping he'll allude to us playing again sometime—even though we haven't even started yet—but he leaves it there. Once his sleeves are rolled up to expose his thick forearms, he crooks a finger.

"Come to me, pet."

His hand is around my throat the moment I get close enough and I stare at him, fighting back panic even as lust throbs through my lower belly.

"You can breathe," he whispers. I can feel his fingertips digging into my neck and am strangely helpless, immobile just from this single, simple grip.

Taking a tentative breath, I realize he's right. I can still breathe.

"Are you going to be a good girl and do as I tell you?" he growls.

Trying to nod, I realize it's impossible. "Yes, Sir," I say in a strangled voice.

"I'm going to hurt you, Sabina," he says, and another bolt of lust punches through my lower belly. "But I'm also going to bring you pleasure unlike any you've ever known. On the condition that you do as you're told. Understood?"

"Yes, Sir." My knees are suddenly weak, and I'm glad he's holding me up.

His free hand drifts down to my chest and he caresses my left breast, scraping it lightly with his fingernails. "Such pretty, taut little nipples," he says, and I tense, expecting him to pinch. Instead, he raises his hand and slaps my breast, hard, still holding me in place by my throat. "Eyes on me. Don't you dare look away."

I fight to keep my focus on his handsome face as he slaps my breast again and again, the sting increasing sharply with each stroke until I don't think I can bear another one, and try to twist away.

"Nuh-uh," he barks. "Did I say you could move?"

"Sorry, Sir," I croak.

Still holding me, he adjusts his position slightly and slaps my other breast, over and over until tears are stinging my eyes.

"What do you say?"

"Thank you, Sir."

"Good girl. Manners are important."

I gasp as he grips my abused breast, squeezing it briefly before sliding his fingertips down my belly, lower and lower until they reach that aching, throbbing place between my thighs.

"Manners will get you rewarded," he whispers, finding my pulsating clit and stroking it so delicately, it takes everything I have not to thrust my hips forward in an attempt to get more friction. "Hmm," his tone is almost conversational, "it seems someone's enjoying herself."

All I can do is whimper as he increases the pressure slightly, his fingertip drawing excruciating circles around that rigid, sensitive nub between my legs.

"Do you like that, pet?"

"Y-yes, Sir."

"I can tell." His expression is cool, almost mocking, which only adds to my humiliation. There he is, fully dressed, while I'm completely naked, writhing helplessly and desperate for more after just a couple seemingly effortless touches. His nails dig cruelly into my clit and I yelp, going up onto my tiptoes in a fruitless attempt to escape him. "But you're not coming yet. Not for a long time…"

He removes his hand and I feel the loss acutely, the sharp pain from his pinch still echoing through my most sensitive place.

Then he moves his face so close to mine that for a moment I think—hope—he's going to kiss me. Instead, he whispers, "And of course, you know not to come unless I say you can."

Jesus. "Yes, Sir."

"Good." He takes a step back and lets go of my throat. I'm glad he takes my arm instead, otherwise I might already have hit the floor. My knees feel like they're made of water. "Let's get you in position so we can have a little fun."

I feel like I'm in a dream as he steers me over to the St. Andrew's Cross and positions me the way he wants me: facing it, my arms and legs spread and cuffed into place.

"Comfortable?" he asks, once he's finished.

"Yes, thank you." I close my eyes, partly glad I can no longer see him, partly disappointed. There's a dull ache between my thighs, and my breasts are still stinging hot from his palms.

"Excellent. Then we can begin."

I barely have time to wonder what will happen next before something thick and heavy thumps across my shoulder blades. Then the same thing strikes my butt. It's a flogger, I realize, but it must be massive, with thick falls and plenty of weight behind it.

Maximus strikes up a rhythm, alternating strokes on my upper back and my ass. I lay my cheek against my right bicep and close my eyes, losing myself in the delicious, thuddy sensations. It doesn't hurt at all; it feels more like I'm being massaged, even when he begins to hit me harder.

I'm limp, liquid, beginning to float...

Whap! A scorching blaze of stinging agony across my asscheeks draws a cry of shock and pain from my lips, and every muscle in my body tenses as if a button had been pushed.

"That got your attention." His sentence is followed by another stroke and I try in vain to squirm away, outraged at being yanked so unceremoniously from my blissful space.

"This is a genuine Louisiana prison strap," Maximus says, searing my flesh with it again and again. "Known to make grown men cry."

I can't breathe; it feels like the skin is being flayed from my buttocks. I twist the chains on the cuffs around my wrists and grip them for dear life.

"Are you crying yet, pet?"

"No!" I gasp, trying to remember to breathe.

"Well, I'm not stopping until you do."

He delivers several more searing strokes and I have no choice but to take them, bound as I am to the cross. The strap must be huge, it feels like he's hitting the same place every time—a broad swath of both my cheeks.

Closing my eyes, I force myself to concentrate. To focus. And slowly, through the agony, I grow increasingly aware of another sensation: a hot, liquid melting between my spread thighs.

"Want some more?" Maximus growls.

"Yes, Sir," I gasp, determined not to give him the upper hand.

If he's surprised, he hides it well. "You didn't say please, pet."

Fuck. Five more strokes burn my ass in breathtaking, agonizingly quick succession before I've even drawn breath to cry, "Please!"

His hand suddenly cupping my sex startles me and I jump, letting out a helpless groan as he grips my whole pussy, grinding his palm against my clit... back and forth. His hand is sliding so easily, my face burns almost as hot as my ass at the thought that there's no hiding my arousal from him.

"Gods, you're wet," he says gruffly. "You really do like pain, don't you?"

His other hand finds my breast and squeezes cruelly, his fingertips digging into the soft flesh.

I'm writhing, moaning, the searing sting in my buttocks only serving to heighten the relentless way he's rubbing my clit against the flat of his hand.

"You're dripping into my palm," he says. "Do you want to come?"

"Yes! Oh god, please, yes, Sir!"

"Not yet." He withdraws his hand and the next minute, he's rubbing those fingers, slick with the proof of my arousal, across my lips and chin. "You smell so good," he growls. "Taste it."

I open my mouth and let him slide two fingers over my tongue.

"Atta girl," he says. "Get them nice and clean."

I suck them then, suddenly wishing they were his cock. He won't be the only one to tease; I can give as good as I get. I'm rewarded with a groan, and resist the urge to grin triumphantly. I want him as desperate for me as I am for—

The man sometimes moves with a speed that defies all logic. I haven't even finished the thought before his fingers have left my mouth and are buried deep up inside my pussy, fucking me roughly, scouring my G-spot with such force that my thighs are shaking.

"Don't you fucking dare come," Maximus orders furiously, "don't you dare until I tell you to, or I swear I'll take a—"

I climax with a helpless shout, my hips bucking so hard that I'm slamming my pelvis against the unforgiving wood of the cross over and over as my pussy snatches at his still-working fingers. The sensation is so intense that I'm glad I'm being held up by the cuffs, and even as I can't stop groaning, a distant part of me is aware that I'm squirting, my juice splashing my thighs...

9

M *aximus*

I DON'T THINK I've been this hard since I was a teenager. Sabina is actually squirting, splattering my arms, shirt, and the floor with irrevocable, irrefutable proof that she defied my order not to come without permission.

Not that she had a choice. If I decide to make a woman climax, then climax she will, regardless of how hard she tries not to, how desperate she is to obey me.

I do love a good head-fuck.

Crouched down behind her as I am, I could easily extend my tongue and lick the taut, shiny, scarlet skin of her abused ass. Her scent is overwhelming, and I can almost taste her shame at not being able to hold back.

She's a fucking delight.

A genuine painslut.

And so much fun to torment.

One night will never be enough time to do all the things I want to her. Hell, I don't think a week would be enough.

Not bothering to hide my smile of triumph, I remove my fingers from her dripping cunt and order her to hold still before allowing myself the luxury of tasting her. Her clit is so swollen and rigid, it feels like a tiny pebble against my tongue. I lap at it briefly, closing my eyes and savoring the musky scent of her desire, the salty and slightly metallic tang of the blood pounding through her sex. I can taste it through her skin and the urge to bite, to allow the delicious elixir to run over my tongue to mingle with her juices, is so overwhelming that I almost lose control.

Almost.

You don't get to be as old as I am without learning to manage yourself, though, so I snap myself out of it, give her clit another hard, lingering lick, and straighten up.

Her chest is heaving, she's breathing raggedly, her whole body trembling and slick with sweat. I don't need to look to know her face is flushed, her eyes glazed.

"You bad little girl," I whisper in her ear. "Not only did you come without permission, you squirted all over yourself... the floor..." I lower my tone, "me."

Her only response is a whimper which makes my balls ache.

"What did I say would happen if you disobeyed me?"

She shakes her head. I want to bring her back—just a little—to make sure she's still capable of safewording if she needs to. And that means making her use her words. "Tell me."

"Y-you'll..." She swallows, her throat working. "P-punish me, Sir."

"And did you disobey me?" I have to fight to hide the smile from my voice.

"Y-yes, S-Sir. I'm s-sorry..."

I allow myself a mocking chuckle as I leave her side for just long enough to extract what I want from my bag. "Oh, pet. You're not sorry yet. But you will be."

The Lexan cane is black, long, and tapers to a point. It leaves delicious marks which last for days. I suddenly have the urge to mark Sabina; a primal desire to leave lingering traces of myself on her delectable body.

"Brace yourself, sweetheart," I tell her, raising the cane. "This is going to hurt."

I snap the rod across the lower, fleshiest part of her ass. It was a decent stroke—not full-force, by any stretch of the imagination, but hard enough to wrench a garbled scream from the beautiful blonde who received it. Gods, but the noises she makes go straight to my groin. A bright scarlet line springs up, stark even against the mottled, hot pink induced by the prison strap. She won't be able to sit down for a few days without thinking of me—a thought I find infinitely pleasing. "Count it and thank me," I tell her coolly.

She's fighting to retain some composure, and I wonder whether she's ever allowed herself to lose control for longer than a few seconds at a time. "One, thank you, Sir," she gasps.

I aim the next one a mite higher up, about an inch above the first. My good aim is one of the many things I pride myself on. To Sabina's credit, her only response is a gasp.

Then, without being prompted, "Two, thank you, Sir."

Suddenly desperate to make her scream, I lay the third across the backs of her thighs, a cold, hard stroke on virginal, as yet unpunished flesh. It must have been excruciating, as it has the desired effect. Sabina throws her head back and howls, "Fuuuck!"

I wonder whether she can hear the delight in my voice

as I put my lips close to her ear. "Tut tut, little pet. What did I tell you about swearing?"

"I'm sorry, I'm sorry, I'm sorry..." It's like a mantra, the words tumbling out of her plump, delectable mouth. She sucked my fingers deliberately earlier, an attempt to regain the upper hand, to make me weak with desire by putting the image of her sucking my cock in my mind. Moreover, it worked, and while I already punished her for it by forcing her to come without my permission—and am punishing her for *that* now—I realize I still want to make her pay for it.

And I will.

"I'll tell you what," I whisper, allowing her to feel my breath on her skin. "You take another six of these without making a sound, and I'll fuck you. Do you want me to fuck you, Sabina?"

Her reply is so quiet, I barely hear it even with my highly developed sensory ability. "What was that? I didn't hear you."

"Please..."

"Say it, Sabina," I order. She hesitates, and I know she's fighting a battle within herself. I slap her ass with all my might, but she's so far gone by now that she barely seems to register it. "Say it." I'm deliberately using the tone of voice I know will have an effect on her.

"Please... fuck... me..."

My cock is rigid, pounding. As much as I want to feel her lips on me there, I know I wouldn't be able to last. Next time. There will be a next time, I've already decided that. If I have to take Sabina home with me and lock her up to ensure it, I will. But first things first.

"You know what?" I'm being cool, almost conversational. "I've decided that I will—fuck you, that is—regardless of whether or not you take these last strokes well. But you're still getting six more with the cane. Now... are you listening?" I wrap her long hair around my fist and yank her head back. The silver crescent moon in the hollow of her throat is jumping in time with her racing pulse.

"Yes, Sir," she gasps.

"If you take these without making a sound, you'll get to come. Maybe once, maybe twice... hell, maybe I'll make you come so often and so hard that you'll beg me to stop. However, if you so much as cry out, you can rest assured that the only one coming tonight will be me. You'll be going to bed with a throbbing, aching, unfulfilled little cunt."

She flinches gratifyingly at the c-word. Another head-fuck. Don't let them swear, but be crass yourself. Some women hate some words and it's always fun to find out which ones react to which.

I slide the cane up the inside of her thigh and between her swollen lips. She rewards me with a gasp when I press it against her most sensitive spot. "Have I made myself clear?"

"Yes, Sir."

"Good girl. Then let us begin." I remove the cane from between her legs, release her hair, roll my shoulders to loosen them, and take up my stance behind her.

It's time to make my mark, to ensure this delightful blonde won't forget me anytime soon.

One of the many advantages of being a vampire is the ability to move insanely fast. We call it *blurring*. I can cross a room in the blink of an eye.

I can deliver six well-aimed, hard strokes of the cane just as fast. And I proceed to do just that, laying three searing, scarlet lines across Sabina's lower buttocks and another three across the backs of her thighs before she even has time to brace herself or draw breath.

Which means the impact of all six hit her at the same

time—and when that happens, I've long since dropped the cane, one of my hands is already between her legs, and the other is clamped tightly over her mouth.

Her scream vibrates through my very being, muffled as it is by my fingers, and even as the pain lights her every nerve ending on fire, her cunt gushes into my palm.

I can't wait any longer. "Come now," I growl, stroking rhythmically over her clit, and she obeys with a helpless groan, which turns into a whimper when I let go of her for long enough to undo my slacks, free my erection, and roll a condom over it before gripping her hips and tugging her into position. She's still coming when I thrust my cock up inside her, her dripping, tight little cunt pulling me in greedily.

Gods, it takes every ounce of the self-control I've honed over centuries not to come the minute I'm all the way inside her. Instead, I focus on wrapping her thick, soft hair back around my fist and tugging her head back to bare her neck. My other hand delves down over her soft lower belly and I find her clit, leaping in time with her heartbeat.

The familiar sensation of saliva flooding my mouth makes my fangs extend and even though I'm not moving yet as I'm giving her a moment to adjust to my size, my cock jerks inside her, making her gasp.

My fingertip is slippery over her clit, sliding back and forth, up and down, changing the pace, direction and pressure often enough that she can't climax.

Yet.

"Such a good girl," I croon, thrusting deeper, pushing her pelvis forward and trapping my forearm against the cross. "You took that so well."

She's panting, trembling, completely gone.

"Six strokes without making a sound means you get a

big reward. I'm gonna make you come so hard. You want to come all over my cock, pet?"

A broken whimper escapes her parted lips.

"I'll take that as a yes. But you have to be good and wait until I say so." I begin to move slowly, withdrawing until only the tip remains before sliding back up inside her. Gods, but I hate condoms. The only thing that would make this better would be if I could feel the velvet walls of her gripping me without that pesky barrier. But I'm wearing it for her protection, not mine. "Can you be a good girl for me one last time, Sabina?"

A mortal wouldn't be able to hear her reply. But I do. "Yes, Sir."

"Your cunt feels so good, pet. I've wanted to fuck you since the first moment I saw you."

Her eyes are closed, her long lashes fluttering against her pale skin. I can hear the blood throbbing through her veins, and my dick jerks again.

Gods, I'm hungry.

Not long now.

"You hold it," I growl, and begin to thrust faster, allowing instinct to take over. My lips find her neck and I lick the spot I'm about to puncture, savoring the salty sweetness of her skin.

She moans as I begin to stroke her clit the way I've discovered she likes it best. Such a responsive little creature. I'm still pumping in and out of her, forcing myself to hold off, relishing the anticipation of what's about to happen.

The deep, dull ache in my balls spreads as they tighten and draw up. Sabina is close, she's shivering in my arms, her pulse pounding in the vein my tongue is tracing circles over. I stroke the rigid nub of her clit two, three more times and then I growl, "Now!"

With a ragged cry, she climaxes beneath my fingertip and I bite down, my fangs puncturing her soft skin. I can't prevent the primal growl I let out as I taste her sweet blood, the metallic, tangy, hot liquid flooding my mouth as I lose myself, fuck her as hard as I can and go over the edge, my cock jerking with my orgasm as I feed. I'm milking her as I sip, drawing out her pleasure, making her climax go on and on as I drink, her tight, sopping little cunt clamping down around my cock over and over again...

10

S*abina*

I'VE NEVER FELT anything even close to what Maximus is doing to me. I'm vaguely aware of a voice sobbing with what could be pain or pleasure—it's hard to tell—and then I realize it's me making that sound.

He's biting my neck but the sharp pain is somehow delicious, and it's radiating throughout my body, spreading along my limbs and pooling in the place between my legs where his huge cock is stretching me beyond what I thought I could handle, or maybe it just feels that way.

I didn't think it was possible for an orgasm to be this intense, or to last this long, but it seems never-ending... wave after wave of pleasure pulsing through my clit, my pussy, my entire being. In fact, I eventually reach a point where I can't take another second of it. I just want it to end. I'm sore, aching, desperate.

"Please," I beg him breathlessly, "please stop. I can't... make it stop."

For a moment, I'm not sure whether he heard me but then he stops stroking my clit and pinches it savagely, pushing me over one final peak—the highest yet. I scream and my knees give out but of course I'm not going anywhere, cuffed as I am to the cross, impaled as I am on Maximus's huge, impossibly thick cock. There's a warm, wet, trickling sensation across my shoulder and then my vision blurs...

When I come to, I need a moment to work out where I am. I'm lying down, wrapped in a soft blanket, and Maximus's handsome face is just above mine, peering down at me.

"Welcome back," he says gruffly.

"What..." I croak, suddenly realizing how dry my mouth is. As if he's read my mind, Maximus holds a bottle of water to my lips and I suck at it greedily, relishing the cool liquid as it soothes my raw throat. I must have done quite a bit of screaming for it to be that sore. Once I've drunk my fill and he's removed the bottle, I try again. "What happened?"

"You passed out," he says. I search his face for any sign of worry but he seems completely unconcerned. In fact, the corner of his wide mouth lifts in a lopsided grin. "I guess you came too hard."

Heat prickles over my face at the memory of what he reduced me to: a begging, shameless, helpless wreck.

God, it was good, though.

I shift, trying to get up, and the deep ache in my backside reminds me of the beating he gave me. Everything's so hazy, part of me feels like I imagined it all, but my body is telling me otherwise. "Was I out long?"

He shrugs. "A few minutes. Long enough for me to get you settled down here."

I have the distinct feeling he's hiding something from me. Come to think of it, I've had that feeling ever since yesterday. But I can't even put it into words, so how could I broach the subject?

"How are you feeling now?" he asks, smoothing my hair back from my forehead.

"Sleepy. But good." Part of me wants to tell him all the other things he's making me feel, but I sense it would be better not to. If he's going to keep secrets, I'd better keep my guard up.

"I think you should come home with me," he says suddenly.

I can only blink at him in response.

"In fact, I won't be taking no for an answer," he goes on.

I find my voice. "Are you serious?"

"Completely."

"Well, you can kiss that idea goodbye," I say, pushing myself into a sitting position, gratified and relieved when he moves back just far enough to let me do so.

He raises a thick eyebrow. "Is that so?"

"Just because we played together, that doesn't make you my keeper. You don't get to give me orders beyond that one session. And besides, why on earth would you suggest such a thing? I'm sure I'll be all right to drive in a little while, maybe after I've had a coffee or two. If not, I'll get an Uber."

His reply takes me completely by surprise. "Is your ex-boyfriend stalking you?"

"What? No! Why would you even think that?" I'm beyond confused now. How did we get from aftercare to this bizarre, inappropriate argument in such a short time?

He holds something up and it takes me a moment to realize it's my cell. "Tell me you did not go through my phone," I snarl, outrage welling hot in my chest at his blatant invasion of my privacy.

"I was worried after your reaction to the text message last night, and then what you said earlier this evening. I care about you, Sabina. I want you to be safe."

"I'm perfectly safe—from Zeke, in any case. *You're* the one going through my messages. That's what I would classify as stalking behavior!" I snap.

Maximus seems irritatingly unperturbed by my outburst. "Why is he warning you to stay away from here then? Has he been here before?"

"I don't know! He just told me never to come here... back when we were still together. Maybe he doesn't like BDSM. Maybe he heard rumors. But he doesn't get to tell me what to do any more than you do!"

"That's where you're wrong," Maximus says coolly. Then, to my absolute astonishment, he scoops me up off the floor, blanket and all, and strides out of the booth.

I'm still completely naked save for my shoes, and grateful for the blanket as we head through the club. "What about my things?" I bleat. "My clothes, my purse... Your bag and jackets..."

Maximus ignores me. Helpless, livid, I stare up at his square jaw, trying to think of a way to reason with him.

"Augustus," he says at length. I turn my head and see the guy who escorted me down the stairs earlier. "If you would be so kind as to gather everything you can find in booth one and bring it to me, I'd be eternally grateful," Maximus tells him.

I take an outraged breath. "I'm perfectly capable of—"

"Certainly," Augustus cuts me off, and then he's gone.

I decide to try another tack. "Sir," I say in my most submissive tone, "I appreciate that you want to take care of me. But there's really no need. Zeke is all bark and no bite. He's mad that I dumped him, and now he's trying to intimidate me to get his own back. I'm not in any kind of danger. Besides, I have a cat at home." Actually, I have an automatic feeder and fountain set up for Felix, so he'd be perfectly fine left on his own for quite some time, but Maximus doesn't need to know that.

"Then we'll stop by your place, feed your cat and pick up some things, and then go to mine."

Jesus, this guy is stubborn. And insanely strong, I realize as I try to struggle. The blanket begins to slip but Maximus's grip on me is impossible to break out of. With infuriating ease, he tucks the blanket back up around me. "I don't need you to take care of me! I'm perfectly fine!"

"Tell me," he says coolly, "what did Zeke's last message to you say?"

"Something again about staying away from here," I mutter. "Something about it being a last warning."

"Wrong," Maximus says. "Seems he texted you again while you were... otherwise occupied."

I close my eyes as the blush creeps over my cheeks. As furious as I am with Maximus, that little reminder of what he just did to me is enough to make another pulse of desire thump through my sex. "And what does the latest message say?" The defeat in my voice is audible and I want to kick myself for it.

"See for yourself." Maximus holds it up for me to read.

You didn't want to listen so you'll have to feel. I'll be waiting for you to come out.

My heart begins to pound. Maximus is not wrong—unlike the other messages, this one does sound more like a direct threat. But I'm not one to run and hide. I can handle

Zeke. I don't need a white knight to come rescue me. They only exist in fairytales, anyway.

In the real world, it's every woman for herself. At least in my experience.

"He's bluffing," I mutter.

"I would hope so," Maximus says. "But as long as there's even just the tiniest chance that he isn't, I'm not letting you go anywhere alone."

"That's a ridiculous notion for a start!" I sputter, outrage once again taking over.

"Here you go, Maximus," a male voice says and I look over to see Augustus has returned, his arms laden with clothing, the toy bag and my purse both slung over his broad, suited shoulder.

Maximus flashes him an apologetic, annoyingly charming grin. "I've kind of got my hands full. Would you be a gent and accompany us to my car?"

"No problem."

"That won't be necessary," I tell Augustus, no longer bothering to hide my anger. "I can carry my things myself. As soon as this oaf puts me down, I'll relieve you of them."

Augustus looks at Maximus and raises a questioning eyebrow. An entire exchange seems to pass between them without either man uttering a single word.

"I don't get a say in any of this?" I snap as Maximus turns and heads for the stairs, Augustus following close behind us.

"Seeing as you just called me an oaf, and you're about to spend quite a bit of time with me—and my toy bag—I would suggest you think very carefully about what you say in the near future," Maximus says softly. "And there's no need to be so angry. I'm only doing my job. I'm looking after you."

"That may have been your job yesterday, when you were on duty," I tell him, "and maybe even just now, after the scene, but like I said before, you're not my keeper or my dom. I'm a grown woman and I'm completely capable of looking after myself. You don't even know Zeke! He'd never do anything to actually hurt me."

"Are you so sure of that?" Maximus is striding up the steps now, as easily as if he weren't carrying anything, let alone my entire body. He's not even out of breath, and for a moment, I'm too impressed to respond.

But I soon shake myself out of that. "Yes, actually, I am sure. Please."

"Sabina." God, the way he says my name makes my breath catch in my throat, even when I'm livid with him. "This is a battle you have lost. You should accept it. No amount of screaming, crying, pleading, wheedling or shouting is going to change it. When you consented to play with me earlier—when you let me *fuck* you—"

To my eternal shame, the way he says that makes another hot rush flood my sex...

"You made me your keeper, at least of sorts," he goes on, apparently unaware of the effect his offhand reminder of what we've just done had on me. "I feel responsible for your welfare."

We've made it through the upstairs bar now and are outside. He pauses to tuck the blanket more securely around me and glances at the sky before striding on in the direction of a side street.

"Imagine if I let you go and something happened to you. I would never forgive myself."

I stop and let that notion sink in for a moment. It's a fair point. Unfortunately.

"What exactly is the plan then?" I ask him, defeated—at least for the time being.

"We'll go to your place, feed the cat, get some things for you to spend the night. Then we'll go on to mine, where Zeke can't possibly find you."

"We don't need to feed the cat," I say in a small voice. "He has an automatic feeder and fountain."

"Even better. Then we can go straight to mine." He gives me a brief squeeze. "Thank you for your honesty."

"I'd still like to pick up some things," I say.

"I have spare toothbrushes and stuff at my house," he tells me. "We can go to your place tomorrow if we need to. Now that we don't have to worry about—what's your cat's name?"

"Felix."

"Now that we don't have to worry about Felix going hungry, I'd rather get straight home. Here, this is my car."

Unbelievable. The man is able to hold me with one arm as he reaches into his pocket and presses the remote. His car is an enormous black Cadillac. I don't know much about makes or models but it looks very new, and very expensive.

"Just throw it all in the backseat, Augustus," Maximus says, tugging open the passenger door and setting me down in the leather seat. I wince as my bruised butt takes my weight, even on the cushioned surface. "Buckle up, pet."

"What about my car?" I bleat, but he shuts the door on my protests and walks around to exchange a few words with Augustus before folding his huge frame into the driver's seat. The car is so big that he has to step up to get in, rather than bend down.

I tug the blanket tighter around myself and let out a huff of frustration. What started as a delicious evening has taken a turn I am absolutely unable to control.

And if there's one thing I hate, it's feeling like I've lost control. I can handle it—enjoy it, even—during a scene, but that's the only exception.

"Where do you live, anyway?" I mutter as he starts the engine and pulls out of his parking spot. His car screams money but for all I know, the repayments on it could be crippling him financially.

"Not far," he says. Then he glances over at me. "And you can stop sulking. Gods, I've never met a woman so unwilling to be looked after."

"Then you've met a whole lot of helpless women," I retort, turning to look out of my window. The lights are getting fewer; we seem to be heading out of the city and towards the mountains.

He lets out a light chuckle. "One or two."

We drive in silence for a while, and I replay the events of the evening in my mind like a movie reel. As infuriating as he's being now, I can't deny that Maximus gave me the best, most intense session of my life, and that's not even counting the sex. I wonder what it would be like if we fucked properly... in a bed, both naked, able to look each other in the eye... and clamp my thighs together at the sudden gush of warmth between them that that thought causes.

Maybe going back to his place isn't such a bad idea after all. Maybe there'll be a round two.

I suddenly find myself praying that there will be... and hating myself for it.

11

M aximus

Sabina is silent for the remainder of the drive back to my mansion in Rattlesnake Canyon. Gods, but she's a stubborn one. Reminds me of Caroline, in a way, and I force that thought from my mind as soon as it appears.

I made her faint intentionally. That way, she didn't notice when I had finally drunk my fill, used my trusty pin to stab my fingertip, and smeared a drop of my blood over the puncture wounds on the side of her neck to stop the bleeding. Vampire blood has healing properties. There are still marks, and there will be for quite a while, but I was able to buy some time. For all she knows right now, she passed out from pleasure and woke up to aftercare.

Until the fight started.

I couldn't help it. She looked so beautiful lying there, so fragile and helpless, and once again my thoughts turned to the fear in her eyes when she received that message yesterday. I'm not normally one to snoop but I had to know for sure whether she really is in any kind of danger.

Since she doesn't have any kind of password lock on her phone, it was easy enough to get in and check. Had I not seen what I saw, I would have tucked it back into her purse, given her aftercare for long enough that she was fully recovered, and sent her on her merry way.

At least, that's what I'm telling myself.

But when I read the messages, I was so glad I'd bothered to look. The contents were bad enough, but when I spotted the little picture of the sender—Zeke, I want to spit his name—I was able to recognize instantly what he is. Something Sabina probably isn't even aware of if they only dated for a few weeks.

Her ex-boyfriend is a fucking dirty shifter. Cheetah, from what I could tell, but that's not the worrying part. Regardless of what she says, I know his type, and they are absolutely capable of carrying out their threats. They're also nearly as possessive of their women as we vampires can be.

It was immediately clear why he'd told her to stay away from the club. There's been a feud between shifters and vampires for the longest time. The bastards have the audacity to call us *leeches*. My fingers tighten briefly on the steering wheel as anger surges within my chest. They roam around in packs, love to fight, and are generally just troublemakers all round. You'd think us non-humans would stick together. It's hard enough to hide superpowers and blend in when we're surrounded by mere mortals, but no. There's been all kinds of wrangling over territory and other nonsense. Not even Lucius making Selene—who's half shifter herself—his queen has completely smoothed things over.

No, I have no time for their kind at all. Selene is all right, we've accepted her—not that Lucius gave us much choice—but as for the rest... The males, especially, are prone to uncivilized behavior: starting fights, squabbling over mates, holding metaphorical pissing contests to prove their dominance. So we vampires try to stay out of their territory, and they stay out of ours... at least for the most part.

If Zeke considers Sabina his mate, however, and has somehow found out that she's now spending time with us vamps, she could be in a lot more danger than she realizes.

Which is why she's in my car, being taken to my house, where she'll be safe from him.

To be honest, I haven't planned much further ahead than that. *Eliminate any immediate threat to start with, worry about the rest later* has always been my motto. And she could be right. He could just be bluffing, hurt pride making him lash out to try and frighten her.

But until I know for sure, I'm not taking any chances.

I glance over at the gorgeous creature in the passenger seat. Her arms are crossed defensively over her chest and she's staring sullenly out of the window. Returning my attention to the road, I attempt to start a conversation. "Are you going to sulk for the rest of the night?"

"I'm not sulking."

I suppress a grin. "You shouldn't lie to me, Sabina. I might make you regret it."

"I couldn't regret anything you did to me now more than I regret agreeing to play with you," she retorts.

Ouch. "That's another lie. You don't regret playing with me. In fact, I bet you'd do it again if I asked you nicely."

She doesn't reply to that, and I grace her with an audible sigh as I turn into my long driveway. Unfortunately, my mansion is less impressive at night, and I never get to enjoy the stunning views over the Catalina Foothills during the day, for obvious reasons. But it's big and comfortable, and fifty acres means I have absolute privacy. I'd love Sabina to be able to explore and enjoy it while I sleep tomorrow but the way she's behaving right now is making it much more likely that I'll have to lock her in somewhere. More's the pity.

The security gate slides open when I hit the button on my remote, and then I roll the car up the remainder of my driveway, pressing another button to open the four-car garage. Right now, I only have one other car—a Rolls Royce, my pride and joy—but that's parked at the other end. As I use this vehicle more often, I reserve the spot right beside the entrance to the house for the Cadillac.

If Sabina is impressed, she's hiding it well. "I guess this place is home," she mutters.

"It is. Well, technically this is just the garage..." I press the remote and the door to the garage slides shut behind us.

"You can't keep me here forever," she blurts out suddenly. "I have my cat, a job, siblings, friends... They'll miss me if I don't turn up on Monday. What you're doing is basically kidnapping."

I'm unable to suppress my short bark of laughter. "What I'm doing, pet, is taking care of you and making sure you're safe. Not that you're displaying a single ounce of gratitude. Now get out of the car, or am I going to have to carry you into the house?"

"I can walk."

By the time I've taken our things from the backseat, she's standing at the door to the house, clutching the blanket around herself like it's a shield. Her long hair is cascading over her shoulders, hiding the puncture marks left by my teeth. Gods, but she tasted better than anything I've had in decades. My cock throbs at the memory. I prowl towards her, backing her up against the door and putting my face so close to hers, I can feel her breath on my lips. "You're not my prisoner, Sabina," I say in a low voice. "You're my guest. I very much enjoyed playing with you. Fucking you. I'd like to do it again."

Her breathing has quickened and her pupils dilate—I can see that even in the semi-darkness of the low garage light. My reminder of how I made her feel earlier is having the intended effect.

"I happen to know Zeke." It's only half a lie. "And I'm worried that he's not just bluffing. I care about you, pet, and that's the only reason why I've brought you here. Once we've made sure you're not in any real danger, if you decide you never want to see me again, that's fine. You can leave, and I'll let you go. In fact, I'll drive you back to your car myself." The mere thought of that actually happening is enough to make a pang of something stab my gut but I ignore it.

"Oh," she says in a small voice.

"So now it's up to you," I tell her. "You can make the best of a bad situation here with me and enjoy the remainder of our time together, or you can dig your heels in and fight me every step of the way. Much less fun, and you know you won't win. So what will it be?"

There's a long, long pause while she thinks. Then, "Enjoy our time together, I guess."

I realize I'm grinning. "Atta girl," I say. "Definitely the right choice. Now, let's go in, shall we?"

~

Sabina

. . .

I'VE ONLY EVER SEEN places like this in the movies. Going up Maximus's driveway alone took what felt like forever. His garage has enough room for a fleet of cars, and now this. I follow him through a huge, impressive hallway and to an enormous kitchen with a vast, square marble island in the center of it. The floor is dark hardwood, the acres of cabinets are mahogany, offset perfectly by the pale beige tiles and marble countertops.

"Would you like something to drink?" he asks, setting his toy bag on the floor, draping both his suit jackets over one of the chairs, and handing me my purse and dress. For a second, I wonder where my panties are, then I remember he put them in his pocket earlier. I put my dress and clutch bag on the kitchen island.

"Something strong," I mutter as my cheeks heat up at the memory.

"You have to be a bit more specific than that." He prowls over to a dining area which is easily as big as the kitchen, heading towards a massive cabinet. "Another gin and tonic?"

"Double, please." I glance at the vast, black windows. The views from here must be spectacular during the day. "How big is this place?"

"Just under thirteen thousand square feet." There's no pride in his voice as he pours a finger or two of whisky into one tumbler and a decent amount of gin into a tall glass. "Tonic's in the fridge."

I stare blankly at the walls of cabinets, wondering which one is hiding the refrigerator.

"Right in front of you. The big one." There's amusement in his tone and I yank the doors open with a little more force than is strictly necessary. Jesus, it's big enough to stash bodies in. "If you want ice, it's—"

"I don't need ice," I interrupt him, tugging the bottle of

tonic out of the fridge and taking the glass of gin from him. "Thank you." This guy's got me so flustered, I can barely tell up from down anymore. My emotions are all over the place: furious one minute, almost incoherent with desire the next.

Bastard.

I slosh some tonic into the gin and take a huge gulp. I suppose this place isn't too bad... for a prison.

"Living room's through here," Maximus says, leading the way. I follow him, my eyes on stalks as I try to take it all in: the sand-colored walls, high ceilings crossed with dark beams, polished hardwood floors, and blatantly expensive furniture and rugs. There are banks of floor-to-ceiling windows everywhere, like shiny black mirrors.

Maximus sinks into a huge, plush sofa and pats the spot beside him with his free hand. "Come sit by me," he says in that dominant growl, and my legs take me toward him as if they have a life of their own.

"How are you feeling, pet?" he says, once I've sat down.

Tired. Confused. Horny. Frustrated. "Fine," I say.

His hand, idly stroking the back of my head, suddenly grips a chunk of hair at my nape and tugs sharply. "What did I tell you about lying to me?"

"I'm sorry," I whimper even as a bolt of desire shoots through my lower belly. The man is a revelation: one touch, and I'm putty in his hands. "I'm... confused, Sir. I'm feeling a lot of things."

"That's understandable." His grip loosens and he resumes stroking me gently. I shiver. "How's your ass?"

Now I'm smiling despite myself. "Sore. Good."

"Good," he echoes. "I did so enjoy hurting you."

Another deep, languid thump reverberates through my core.

"And you took it so well. Spread your thighs."

My sex must be raw, and I'm certain even the slightest touch now would be excruciating, but I still find myself obeying his command. It's like I have no free will around him.

"Good girl."

I'm holding my breath, waiting for his touch, but nothing happens. Instead, he takes a sip of his whisky, his other hand still playing with my hair. Feeling stupid, I begin to close my knees again but his growl stops me dead.

"Keep them open until I tell you otherwise."

It's humiliating, sitting beside him with my thighs splayed, but it's somehow also supremely erotic. I drain my gin and tonic to hide how aroused I am. Maximus might be bossy, and strange, and extremely secretive, but he is easily the sexiest man I've ever met. A mere raised eyebrow from him turns me on more than hours of foreplay with anyone else.

"You smell so good," he whispers. "And so wet. I can smell your excitement from here."

My cheeks are on fire and I close my eyes, wanting to hide from his scrutiny but aware that there's nowhere to go.

"I wonder, pet... are you still wet from before, or is it turning you on again to sit here on my couch, wearing nothing but a blanket, your thighs spread like a hungry, greedy little slut who's desperate for cock?"

The moan escapes my lips before I can stop it. His crude words make me feel ashamed and aroused at the same time, and I hate myself for it.

"You want me again, don't you?" His growl is like a caress. "That sensitive place between your legs is sore and achy but it's also swollen and throbbing, isn't it? Desperate for my fingers... my tongue... my cock..."

I open my eyes and watch him as, with deliberate slowness, he finishes his whisky and sets the tumbler on the coffee table. Taking my empty glass from my hand, he puts that down as well. Then his fingertips are tracing the top of my thigh. I let out another helpless moan.

"Say it, sweet Sabina," he murmurs. "Tell me what you want."

I close my eyes again—anything to hide from his penetrating stare—and shake my head. I can't say it. I can't.

The pinch he delivers to my inner thigh is so savage that I gasp and jerk back.

"I won't ask you again," he snarls.

"Please," I whisper, not even sure what I'm asking for. *Mindless with need* is an expression I've heard and read about so many times, but I never really understood it.

Until now.

"Please... what?" He's stopped stroking my hair now and is gripping the nape of my neck. The scrap of skin on my inner thigh that he's got trapped between his nails is burning almost as hot as my face.

"I don't know," I moan. "I can't... I can't think straight right now."

He tuts sympathetically, and I gasp as he takes his nails out of my flesh. "Poor little pet. Shall I help you?"

I nod.

"You can do better than that. Remember your manners."

"Yes, Sir. Please help me."

His touch is so light at first that I'm not sure whether I'm imagining it. Then he increases the pressure, ever so slightly, and I realize that yes, he really is tracing circles over my clit. I'm already trembling; rhythmic pulses of indescribable pleasure are thumping through my pussy at his expert caress. His grip on my neck is keeping my upper body immobile but I'm grinding my hips, trying to control the way he's stroking me.

"Keep still, pet," he says softly. "Don't move, and don't make a sound."

It takes every ounce of self-control I have to obey but I force my body to relax.

"Atta girl," he murmurs, his fingertip still moving relentlessly, as inexorable as a metronome. My clit feels huge, my pussy strangely empty. I realize I want his cock back inside me more than anything I've ever wanted in my life. "Just sit there and take it," he continues, "be a good girl for me. And when I tell you to, you're going to come for me—you're going to come good and hard for me—and you're not going to move or make a sound, otherwise I will take a birch to your thighs, bring you back to the edge of orgasm, and tie your hands to the bed without letting you come. I don't think you'd like to spend the night writhing helplessly, your ass and thighs burning almost as hot as your clit, desperate for release... would you?"

Sweet Jesus. His threat actually makes me gush a little; I can feel the trickle slip from my pussy and slide down over my asshole. I'm about to shake my head, to say *No, Sir*, but then I remember his instructions not to move and realize I'm being tested.

His chuckle tells me I passed. "You're a smart little one, aren't you?" His fingertip slides down between my labia, swirls briefly in my slick juice, and then slides back up to resume its now slippery brushing of my throbbing, rigid bud. "You're so fucking wet, Sabina. I love how responsive you are. I loved the feel of you coming over my cock. I want to fuck you again later. Would you like that? Maybe I'll put you on your knees and make you choke on it before I plunge deep, deep inside your tight, wet, needy little cunt..."

I'm biting my lower lip to stop myself from crying out, his muttered threats and promises washing over me like a litany of pleasure. I'm trembling with the effort not to move as he keeps me on the edge, keeps talking, keeps teasing...

His hand on the back of my neck feels like a brand.

"You're going to come now," he goes on, "and you're going to remember what I said will happen if you so much as move a fucking muscle or even breathe too loudly. You understand me?"

I gush again at his words, then he increases the pressure on my rigid nub just enough to tip me over the edge. Hot, pulsating tingles thump through my core, starting at the spot his fingertip is massaging and radiating out, my pussy contracting again and again as he croons in my ear, coaxing me, drawing it out in that expert, infuriating way of his.

"Good girl, shhh, that's it, come hard for me, don't stop, don't you dare fucking stop now..."

I'm shaking uncontrollably, gripping the blanket around me for dear life as he pushes me on and on, desperate for him to increase the friction just a tad more, just enough to let me finish completely, for this agonizing, ecstatic torment to end.

"You're so beautiful when you're coming, pet, I don't think I could ever tire of the sight. That's why I like to make it last. It's your own fault. I wonder how long we could draw this out for? It's an amazing sensation, isn't it, but at some point it must become excruciating..."

The words leave my lips without conscious thought. "*Please*, Sir! *Makeitstopmakeitstopmakeitstop*..."

For the life of me I don't know how he does it, how he could possibly wring these sensations out of me or know his way around my body so much better than I do, but he changes the way he's touching me and there's one last crescendo of pulse-pounding, pussy-tightening pleasure before it at last begins to ebb. All the tension drains out of me and I slump back against his hand on my neck, exhausted. Spent. Defeated.

Maximus's voice brings me back to the present. "Oh dear." His tone is infuriatingly conversational, as if I weren't sitting in a veritable puddle of my own arousal, as if my entire sex weren't still throbbing with the aftermath of the longest orgasm of my life. "I warned you what would happen if you made a sound."

12

M *aximus*

GODS, but Sabina is stunning when she comes. I drew it out for as long as I could to relish every second of her pleasure, taking in every tiny detail: the blush creeping up her neck and face, the vein thumping in her neck, the trembling of her round, full thighs.

I was also curious to see how long she could take it before she broke. I figure the only way I can tie her up for the day without arousing any suspicion is by making it a punishment, and she played right into my hands.

I seem to be hiding my smile a lot around her.

Now she's gazing up at me with those huge, dark blue eyes, her pink-tipped breasts heaving with every breath.

"I asked you a question," I growl, and she flinches.

"S-sorry, Sir. You said you would punish me."

"Very good. And what did I say would the punishment be?"

She repeats it slowly, as if under duress. Which I suppose she is, in a way. "You... You would take the birch to me, bring me to... to the point of orgasm, and then you'd... tie me to the bed."

Actually, I'd love to fuck her again but sunrise is creeping ever closer and I'm getting tired. "Good girl," I tell her. "And why am I doing that?"

She closes her eyes and I don't miss the way her hands fist the blanket. "I-I made a noise."

"You begged me to make you stop coming, pet," I tell her. "Loudly. After I specifically told you not to move or make a sound."

"I'm sorry, Sir." She's actually hanging her head now, and a pang of something surges through my chest. Gods, what is it about her?

"No need to apologize. I'm about to make you atone," I say in a low voice. "Stand up."

Still clutching the blanket, she gets to her feet, wobbling a little. She has stamina, I'll give her that. I rise, too, and put a steadying arm around her shoulders.

"Do you—" Her voice comes out as a croak and she clears her throat before trying again. "Could I have a shower first?"

"Only if it's very quick. Let me show you to your room."

If she's surprised by the way I refer to it as her room rather than mine, or ours, she doesn't show it. Then again, she's probably exhausted. As am I.

I lead her out of the lounge, up the stairs, and to my favorite guest bedroom. It's done up in different shades of blue and lavender, and the views during the day are simply awe-inspiring.

I've only ever seen them in photographs.

All my bedrooms have ensuite bathrooms, and I lead Sabina into the one adjoining this room. There's a large Jacuzzi tub and a walk-in shower with a variety of shower heads—rainfall, waterfall, massage. It's plenty big enough for two people but as much as I'd like to get in there with her, we simply don't have the time. "Towels and washcloths are in here," I say, tapping a cupboard. "Spare toothbrushes and toothpaste in this drawer. Shampoo, conditioner, body wash... anything else you might need are in this one. Please be quick. You have fifteen minutes. Every minute after that will earn you another five with the birch. On your thighs."

She lets out a half-whimper, half-groan, and my cock throbs at the sound. She really is a little painslut—a genuine one. I love that.

"I'll leave you to it," I tell her. "Remember, you have fifteen minutes—I will make you regret every second you're late."

"Yes, Sir."

I don't miss the click of the lock turning the moment I've shut the door behind me. Now I'm finally able to grin openly. As if locking the door could keep me away. Still, if it makes her feel more secure for the time being, I'll allow it.

Her time limit is mine, too, so I make haste to my bathroom and take a lightning quick shower myself. Then I dress casually in a black sleeveless t-shirt and black sweatpants, leaving my feet bare. I'm not a fan of suits, and generally only wear them at the club.

With minutes to spare, I return to the room I've designated as Sabina's. I place a huge glass of water on the nightstand—alcohol is so dehydrating for humans—and the birch I've selected on the bed, so it will be the first thing she sees when she enters. The king-size bed has clean sheets on it and I've already secured my softest ropes to the wrought-iron headboard.

I don't regret what I am very often. I miss the sun, and it's a shame I never get to enjoy the views from my house during the daytime. Other than that...

But now, strangely, I find myself wishing I were a mere mortal. I could have joined sweet Sabina in the shower, taken her once more, then gone to sleep beside her, holding her close, instead of being forced to hide the truth by tying her up and retreating to my dark basement boudoir. I glance at the glass of water I set out for her, the sour tang of guilt on my tongue at the knowledge of what I'm about to do.

Drugging a woman is morally reprehensible, I know that, but I simply cannot risk her waking up too early. Tied to the bed, she'll be unable to drink, eat, or go to the bathroom, and I don't want her to suffer that way for a moment longer than absolutely necessary. So I slipped a little something into the water I'm about to make her drink. It's tasteless, odorless, and very effective. If everything goes according to plan, she will wake up at around sunset and simply feel like she had a long, deep, dreamless sleep. There will be no time for her to slip out of her bonds—whenever I tie a woman up and leave her alone, I use a special knot which can be undone easily if you find the right place to tug, although I've never yet met one who figured that out, or needed to—or for her to go exploring and wonder where the hell I am.

The bathroom door opens and she emerges in a cloud of steam. I breathe in the sweet, hot scent of her skin and the grapefruit shower gel she must have used. A plain white towel is wrapped around her body, and her damp hair trails over her creamy shoulders.

I fucking love the way her eyes widen when she spots first me, then the birch lying on the bed beside me.

"Did you find everything?" I ask her.

"I did. Thank you."

"You're lucky," I continue, "you just made it. A minute longer, and I would have had to punish you more. Now, come here."

She's tentative as she obeys, her movements slow, but graceful. "I'm about to tie you to the bed. Is there anything else you need to do first?" I mean this is her last chance to use the facilities, and hope I'm not forced to elaborate, but she's smart and deduces my meaning.

"No, Sir. I just went."

"Good girl. Drop the towel, drink some of that water, and lie down."

I'm half expecting a fight but she obediently lays the towel over a nearby chair then drains half the glass—which should be enough—and lies down on her back, letting out a little groan when her ass takes her weight. The sound, as always, goes straight to my cock.

I marvel at how slender her wrists are as I fasten them to the headboard with two good lengths of soft rope, careful not to make her bonds too loose or too tight. She's being much more compliant than I thought she'd be, and I wonder whether it's exhaustion or something else. Perhaps she's realized that there's no point in fighting me.

After all, I always win.

"Is that comfortable?" I ask, gazing down at her stunning, naked form.

"Yes, Sir."

"You can turn onto your side or your belly if you want to?"

She rolls over experimentally. "Yes, Sir."

"Good. On your back for now, pet."

Once she's in the correct position, I pick up the birch rod and whip it through the air a couple of times, suppressing a smile at the expression on her beautiful face. There's fear, certainly, but it's mixed with not a little desire.

"Lift your legs up, there's a good girl. Straight up in the air, feet together. Keep your knees relaxed."

She's supple, and does what I tell her without any apparent effort. Regardless, I wrap my free hand around her ankles to hold her in position.

Her ass is still a hot pink, the welts from the Lexan cane slightly puffy. Her cunt, peeping tantalizingly at me from between her closed thighs, is also still swollen, like a ripe guava. I feel the sudden urge to bite into it. Instead, I lick my lips.

"Why am I doing this?" I say, slipping into my dominant tone.

She closes her eyes and lets out a groan. "Please, Sir, can we just get it over with?"

She's barely finished the sentence before I've applied the birch to her abused buttocks, a swift, hard stroke which makes her scream. "Shall we try that again?"

"B-because I w-wasn't silent when I c-came," she whispers, gratifyingly cowed.

"Better. Are you ready?"

"Yes, Sir."

"Brace yourself, pet. This is going to hurt. You can scream all you like—nobody can hear you."

Holding her legs up with my left hand, I whip the backs of her thighs with my right, applying short, sharp thwacks of the birch up one side and down the other, extending the pattern of fine scarlet lines right up to her knee hollows.

Sabina screams continuously, almost as if I ordered her

to, gyrating her hips in a futile attempt to get out of my way. I do love the birch; its appearance is so deceptive. I barely have to flick my wrists to get the desired effect, and even though it barely makes any noise on impact, the sting it delivers is severe.

I don't have to whip her hard or for very long to achieve the results I want, and the whole thing is over in a couple of minutes. Still holding her ankles, I admire my handiwork and feel my nostrils flare as I catch the unmistakable scent of her arousal.

"There there," I say soothingly, "it's all over. You did so well. I think you deserve a reward. Spread those legs for me, knees to your chest, there's a good girl."

She's stopped screaming and is panting now, and although I was planning to tease her using only my fingers, greed overcomes me. Once I've let go, she does as she was told, splaying herself wide open by spreading her legs and bending her knees.

Without further ado, I bury my tongue in her sweet, hot cunt.

Gods, but the girl is wet, and my cock is rigid in my pants as I eat her pussy like a ripe peach, her juice and my saliva dribbling down my chin. Her clit is like a little marble on my tongue and I suck and lick it hungrily, cruelly gripping the backs of her abused thighs to hold her in place as I devour her. I can smell her blood through her soft skin, and the resulting deep, dull ache in my groin only serves to anger me—she has no right to affect me this way.

She's close, her whole body is trembling, and I slide my tongue as deep inside her as it will go before giving her one more long, lingering lick right up to her clit. Then, reluctantly, I release my hold on her and stand up, wiping my chin.

"I think that's enough," I say. "If you're a good girl, I'll finish this once you've woken up."

Sabina is writhing, twisting in her bonds, her thighs still splayed, reduced to a begging, helpless, lustful wretch. It's so fucking hot to watch, I wish I had time to plunge my cock inside her.

Later.

"You can lower your legs now," I tell her.

"Please," she moans. "Please, Sir. I'll never be able to sleep..."

"Legs down." My growled order brooks no argument and, with obvious reluctance, she complies. I tug the sheet up to cover her, then bend and press a kiss to her forehead. "Good girl. Sweet dreams."

"Wait, where are you going? You're not really going to leave me here, tied to the bed?" There's an edge of panic in her voice, and I feel a pang of regret.

"I won't be far, sweetheart. Get some rest now." Without giving her a chance to reply, ignoring her whimpers, I switch off the main light but leave the bedside lamp on, just in case she wakes up. All my drapes are blackout curtains, so she'd be hard-pressed to see anything even if she wakes up during the day. Suppressing a sigh, I leave the room.

It's almost sunrise, I've only just made it, I think as I make my way down to the basement where I must hide from the deadly sun, as I have done now for countless centuries.

I'm tired, horny, and drained, and yet the echoes of Sabina's whispered pleas follow me down...

13

*S*abina

I JERK AWAKE, filled with confusion as to where I am. Trying to push a sticky strand of hair off my face, I realize my hands are tied to the headboard, and it all comes back to me in a rush. I'm at Maximus's house. We played together, he fucked me, then he took me home. Turning my head, I'm shocked to see he isn't lying beside me. Surely he didn't leave me here by myself for... how long was I asleep? I glance at the window but the thick curtains give nothing away—not even the slightest chink of daylight is to be seen.

Licking my lips, I realize how thirsty I am, and my gaze is drawn to the half-full glass of water on the nightstand. I do my best to reach it but unfortunately the rope Maximus tied me with is too short.

Where is the asshole, anyway?

I feel weirdly groggy, almost like I'm hungover, but I only

had two gin and tonics last night over the course of several hours, so it can't be that. I try to make my body move, to kick off the sheet, but it takes a huge amount of effort and I soon give up. Instead, I force myself to take some deep breaths, fighting back the rising panic.

I'm in a virtual stranger's house, tied to a bed. Naked. My head is foggy. Did he drug me? Surely not. A creep like Ethan would stoop so low, but not Maximus. He's a sadist, definitely, and dominant to the bone, but he's also demonstrated a caring, solicitous side. He works in security, for god's sake. He protects women for a living.

That would be the perfect cover, a little voice tells me, but I decide to ignore it. No, he's probably in the bathroom, or down in the kitchen making us something to eat. I don't really feel hungry, but I'd just about murder someone for a coffee.

The minutes tick by as I lie there, my mind racing. Nobody could need that long in the bathroom. Nor would it take such a long time to grab a bite to eat or make coffee. Where is he?

I shift in the bed and the ensuing ache in my butt reminds me of our session. An instant pang of desire shoots through my lower belly at the memory, my clit suddenly beginning to throb. I can't remember the last time anyone had this kind of sexual effect on me. I thought I would die when he licked me to the very brink of orgasm before leaving me to lie awake, desperately horny and craving the solace of sleep.

Fortunately, despite my fears, I had passed out fairly quickly. Now, though, my nerve endings are all roaring back to life. *Great*, I think. *Now I'm thirsty, aching* and *horny.*

And I'm tied to the bed so I can't do a damn thing about any of it.

I tug experimentally at the ropes around my wrists, twisting my head to get a better view of the knots. I discover I'm actually able to put my hands together, and immediately make use of that advantage by fiddling with the knot on my left wrist.

This is like some cheap horror movie, I find myself thinking as I yank at the soft rope. If I do manage to get myself free, I'll probably find something to wear, go downstairs, and promptly discover a human head in the fridge.

First Zeke, then Ethan, now this. Is there no sane, normal guy left anywhere in the world? Have they really all already been paired up?

At least my focus on untying myself is distracting me from the pulsing between my legs.

"Come on," I encourage myself, feeling the rope loosen slightly. I'm going on touch rather than sight, as I can't keep my head twisted at the right angle to see what I'm doing without getting a crick in my neck. Then my fingertips discover a little loop which seems to be out of place in the otherwise neat knot. I give that a little tug, and almost groan with relief when the entire knot unravels immediately. I should have paid more attention in Girl Scouts; I might have worked it out sooner. With one hand free, I roll over onto my belly and find the loop on the knot around my right wrist. Sure enough, pulling that unravels the last thing binding me to the bed.

Thank fucking Christ. I sit up, clutch my head in a vain attempt to relieve the sudden pounding in my temples, and reach for the glass of water, draining it in a few greedy swallows. Then I swing my legs over the side of the bed, wincing as my sore butt and thighs slide across the sheet, and get unsteadily to my feet.

Yanking back the drapes, I blink against the glaring

sunlight. Then, when my vision returns, I gasp at the view I'm presented with. Nothing but stunning Arizona mountains as far as the eye can see. Not another house in sight; just nature at its most raw and beautiful. Lucky, lucky Maximus to be able to enjoy this on a daily basis. I don't know why he bothers with curtains, it's not like anybody would be able to see in, even at night with the lights on.

My bladder decides to wake up then, and I mince gingerly into the ensuite to take care of that. After washing my hands, I smooth my hair back from my face and flick it behind my shoulders before examining my reflection.

I do not look my best. My eyes are bloodshot. My mascara is clumpy, and I lick my finger to wipe the smudges from beneath my lower lashes. Then something else catches my eye: a mark not unlike a bruise on the side of my neck. It must be from when he bit me during the session last night. I can't remember the last time I had a love bite—not since I was a teenager, in any case—and I lean closer to the mirror to get a better look.

The blood turns to ice in my veins.

Surely not, I think, my heart beginning to pound twice as fast. *It can't possibly be what it looks like.*

There are two puncture wounds starkly visible within the bruise. They're exactly the right size and shape to be...

No, you're being ridiculous, I tell myself. Vampires don't exist outside of novels and movies. Maybe he nipped me accidentally with his teeth while he was sucking my neck— but those marks would be different. Human teeth are blunt. They leave very different impressions. Whereas these... I'm looking at two perfect holes, not unlike those left by a snake bite, only farther apart.

Unable to stop myself, I prod the area, gasping at the sudden, sharp sting. He was biting me for a long time—god, it felt good—but surely that was just a coincidence. Yes, I was coming so hard my knees almost gave way, but even so I'm pretty sure I would have noticed him drinking my fucking blood.

Only I passed out. He could have done it then.

No. Absolutely not. I always did have an overactive imagination, and this just proves it.

Then where is he? I can't help asking myself. *Why are you in what's obviously a guest room and not his room? Isn't it customary for a man to actually sleep in bed with you when you spend the night at his place? Did he drug you and tie you up so you'd sleep until sunset and be none the wiser?*

Is that even a real thing—vampires having to hide from sunlight?

Before I drive myself absolutely insane with these thoughts, I decide to take action. Step one: find something to wear. There's no closet in the guest room but I remember leaving my dress downstairs in the kitchen. Until I get down there, I'll just have to use the towel slung over the chair. Picking it up, I wrap it around myself, grateful for the protection even though it's flimsy.

Holding my breath, my heart hammering in my chest, I tiptoe to the door and open it furtively. A quick glance down the vast hallway confirms there's nobody around, so I head down the stairs and into the kitchen. To my absolute relief, my dress and purse are exactly where I left them. I waste no time in dropping the towel and tugging the dress over my head, then rummage through my bag for my phone.

Crap. It's dead.

Unable to suppress a groan of fear and frustration, I lean on the counter and try to corral my thoughts. I don't have my phone. I don't have my car, and I'm out in the Foothills somewhere. I'd have to walk for miles just to get off his bloody property, and then a lot farther to get back to civilization.

How stupid was I to get myself into this predicament?

Only Maximus didn't really leave me with much choice. And he was so unbelievably charming.

It's a shame he's a vampire.

I have to smile despite myself. There's probably a perfectly reasonable explanation for everything. I could just make myself comfortable, explore this vast, lush mansion, and wait for him to reappear, which he'll probably do soon —after the sun sets, at the very latest, I think wryly.

You're going crazy, Sabina. A sudden hope that I'm dreaming overwhelms me and I give my forearm a savage pinch.

Nope. Still in his kitchen. Still no escape.

Closing my eyes, I tap my fingertips against my forehead and force myself to think. I don't have my car, that's true, but there are two in his garage. I could take one of them and drive myself back to Club Toxic. Technically, it wouldn't be stealing—he works there, and I could drop off or mail the keys back to him later. Provided I can find them.

And that the garage door isn't locked.

Why are you in such a hurry to get away? a little voice asks me. *He hasn't hurt you—at least, not beyond what you consented to.* My clit roars back to life at the thought of his hands on my body, his low, dominant tone in my ear, his tongue driving me to the absolute brink...

If I manage to somehow borrow one of his cars without his consent and get home, one thing is certain: I will never, ever feel any of that again. Maximus would be beyond pissed.

And while I'm perfectly content being single, I can't get over the way my body reacts to him. It's like a drug high, and

I want more. A lot more. I want to know how he kisses, how his cock tastes; I want more of that exquisite torture he can dole out so effortlessly.

Am I really ready to give up the best sex of my life just because I woke up without him, and now have some ridiculous notion that he's not human?

My fingertips slide to the side of my neck and I wince as I encounter the bite mark. It's not just a notion, though. I have tangible, visible proof. And while I agreed to play with him and even have sex with him, I do not recall a discussion about being his dinner.

The bark of laughter which escapes my lips is on the verge of hysterical, and I suddenly feel woozy. I just need to sit down for a moment. Get my bearings. Not make any hasty decisions.

Heading to the den we were in earlier, I allow my weak knees to give way and sink into the plush depths of the sofa. The view in here is just as spectacular as in the bedroom, but my eyelids feel so heavy.

God, I'm tired.

I'll just doze for a few minutes, then I'll pull myself together and come up with a plan. Maybe I'm even still in bed and this is just a dream after all...

14

M *aximus*

MY FIRST THOUGHT upon waking is Sabina. Gods, I hope she's all right. I hope she only just woke up and is now blinking groggily, the memories of this morning slowly coming back to her. I wonder if she's still wet, and my cock twitches at the thought. *Perhaps she's still asleep*, I think as I leave my basement and bound up the stairs, taking them two at a time in my haste to reach her. I could wake her by sliding my dick deep inside—

I blink, my brain unwilling to acknowledge what I'm seeing. The drapes have been yanked back and the bed is empty. The glass on the nightstand is empty. The whole fucking room is empty.

"Sabina? Pet?" I force myself to sound casual as I glance inside the ensuite and see no trace of her. "Where are you?"

She can't be far, I tell myself. We're miles away from

anywhere. She doesn't have a car. She wouldn't know my address, so calling an Uber or a cab would be out, surely?

I begin to search methodically, wondering why I have to have such a big damn house. Once I've ascertained she's not anywhere on the second floor, I go down to the first, rubbing my head compulsively as I check the kitchen, the lounge…

She's curled up on the sofa, wearing her rumpled dress from last night, her feet still bare. I flick on a nearby lamp and she gives a jerk, snapping awake just as I realize what must have happened. She woke up thirsty, somehow managed to find the release loops on the knots I used, drank the rest of the water, and made it this far before passing out again.

"Sabina," I say softly.

She spots me then, and the expression of absolute anguish, fear and betrayal on her face turns my blood to ice. "Maximus," she says coldly. "I'd like to go home please."

In a moment I'm by her side, desperate to pull her against me but somehow sensing that I'm not welcome to touch her right now. "What's the matter?"

"What's the matter?" There's a shrill edge to her voice and she struggles to sit upright, every fiber of her being straining to lean as far away from me as she can. "Where have you been all day?" She indicates the black windows. "Literally *all day*? Did you really tie me to the bed and leave me completely alone? I thought it was a game. I thought you'd join me once I was asleep."

"Listen, pet," I begin, wondering how on earth to explain. This is why I don't ever take girls home. For this exact fucking reason.

"Don't *listen, pet* me!" There's fire and defiance in her beautiful blue eyes now, and again I have to suppress the urge to reach for her. "I know what you are," she says quietly. "You can stop pretending. And it's fine—well, no, it's not fine, actually, but if you just take me home right now, I won't tell anyone. Your secret will be safe with me."

I school my features to give nothing away as I absorb this little statement. "What I am?"

"Yes." She pushes the long blonde hair off her neck and indicates the place where I bit her. A cold dread settles in my gut. "You're a vampire, aren't you? And you fucking bit me!" Then she lets out a shrill, almost hysterical laugh. "I can't even believe these words are coming out of my mouth!"

Every available option open to me flashes through my mind at lightning speed and I evaluate them one by one, considering the consequences. Wipe her mind. Deny it and give some excuse for the marks. Kill her. That last option is an automatic thought because for centuries, it was the only way to guarantee my own survival. But no. We're not in the Dark Ages anymore. Besides, I like her, even when she's staring at me with unadulterated horror on her exquisite face.

"Yes," I say slowly. "You're right. I'm a vampire."

Even though she suggested it first, my confirmation seems to shock her and her mouth drops open. "Really?"

"I won't lie to you, Sabina. I'm sorry you found out this way. First of all, I want to assure you that I would never hurt or harm you, and second, I'd very much appreciate the chance to explain."

"And then you'll take me home?"

"If you still want to go."

Another shrill laugh. "If I still want to go? What's the alternative?"

I shrug. "I'm the same guy I was yesterday."

"No you're not! You're fucking *dead*!"

Ignoring the barb, I reach out and place a hand on her

bare knee. She flinches but doesn't push me away. Promising sign. "Let's discuss this like reasonable adults, shall we? I'll answer any questions you have but first, is there anything you need?"

Her eyes, when she raises them to my face, have lost some of the fear. But she's biting her bottom lip. "I don't suppose you have any coffee?"

I have to suppress a chuckle. It was the last thing I expected her to say, and yet I don't want her to think I'm making light of the situation. "I absolutely have coffee. Anything else?"

She looks down. "And I need the bathroom."

"Nearest one is just down the hall, second door on the left." I jerk my chin to indicate the direction. "I'll be in the kitchen when you're ready." My hand slides off her knee as she gets unsteadily to her feet. "Or do you need me to escort you?" I don't want her falling and hurting herself.

"No, I'm fine, I can take care of myself," she snaps, turning her back on me and heading towards the hall.

I close my eyes against the sudden pang in my chest. How many times did Caroline say that to me, in that exact same tone and with the exact same inflection? Only it was a lie. In the end, she couldn't take care of herself. I couldn't—

No, I tell myself firmly. The past is past, there's no going back. I need to concentrate on the present. Sabina has discovered my secret, and I need to work out how to handle things from here on out.

Making my way into the kitchen, I switch on my coffee machine and select a couple of mugs as the rhythmic crunch of grinding beans fills my ears. The machine was an expensive purchase, especially for one who lives alone and doesn't actually need to eat or drink anything—aside from blood, of course—to survive, but I've developed quite a taste for the stuff. I simply need to make sure it's filled with coffee beans and water, and it does all the rest of the work for me.

As I'm waiting for the beep which tells me the water is hot enough, I lean back against the counter and spot Sabina's bag lying on the island. Her phone is right beside it. I pick it up and realize the battery's dead.

"Snooping again?" says a cold voice, and I turn to see her standing a few feet away, her arms crossed defensively over her chest.

Drat.

"Do you have a charger in that little purse of yours?" I ask her.

"No."

"Didn't think so. There's a Qi over there." I point to the corner, where I always keep it plugged in. "You can just put your phone on it and it will charge, if it's a new enough model."

"Oh. Thanks." Grudgingly, she plucks her cell from my hand and wanders over to lay it on the flat, round charging pad.

My machine beeps. "Coffee's almost ready." I place the first mug under the spout and hit the button. "Do you take cream or sugar?"

"Just cream, thanks."

Under her wary, watchful eye, I prepare two large mugs of coffee and put some cream in hers. I prefer mine black. "I think we should sit down," I tell her, once she's taken a big sip.

"All right."

The kitchen opens out to a large dining area with a table and six chairs. I'm suddenly aware of how ridiculous my home must seem to someone like her. To live alone in a place big enough for not one, but several families. Truth be told, it's not the size of the place that drew me. I could do without most of the rooms—there are several I barely ever use. My housekeeper comes in weekly but other than that, when I am here, I'm alone. And as I spend most of my nights at Toxic, I spend the majority of my time at home in the basement. That's why I picked this house. It has a basement perfectly suited to my needs, and its location is ideal. Fifty acres ensures a great deal of privacy.

Sabina pulls out one of the chairs and sits down, clutching her coffee with both hands. Once I'm seated opposite her, she settles her frank, blue gaze on me and lets out a little huff. "Go on then," she says. "Explain."

"What do you want me to explain?" I counter, unable to suppress the sudden urge to tease her just a tiny bit. She rewards me with an exasperated sigh.

"Everything! I don't know anything about vampires except for what I've seen and read about in movies and books. Are you really dead? Do you really have to keep away from the sun?" Her voice catches and her fingers slide to her neck without any apparent conscious thought. "Did you really drink my blood? Is that why I passed out?"

A wave of sympathy washes over me but I take a sip of my coffee instead of reaching for her. "That's not why you passed out," I say slowly, "but yes, I did... drink from you. I couldn't help it. You were just..." I trail off, not sure whether it would be appropriate at this juncture to tell her how delicious she is.

"If not from that, then why did I faint?"

"From pleasure," I tell her coolly, and she scoffs. "It's true. When we bite, our fangs release a kind of pleasure serum into the vict—into your bloodstream. You were already coming. It was too much pleasure for you to take, so you passed out."

"Wow." She shakes her head. If she caught me almost referring to her as a victim, she very sensibly decided not to address it. Good girl. Sabina narrows her eyes and stares me down. "So how old are you?"

I realize I'm rubbing the back of my head again and force myself to stop. "I was thirty-five when I was turned."

"Turned. You mean when you died and became a vampire?"

I nod.

"And when was that, exactly?"

I sigh. "During a battle. We were fighting Visigoths. I was a centurion."

Sabina blinks rapidly, and I can actually see her doing the calculations in her head. "You're kidding," she says quietly. "Your name is actually Maximus because you're actually, *literally* Roman? But that would make you well over a thousand years old!"

"Just over 1600."

She leans back in her chair, the shocked disbelief evident in her eyes. "Fuck," she says. "Fuck."

"Language," I say automatically, and she graces me with a glare.

"I think, *Sir*," she says coolly, "with all due respect, finding out the guy you just played with and had sex with is actually a dead centurion vampire who's been going around drinking people's blood for sixteen centuries is the kind of exceptional circumstance in which you should be allowed to swear."

I bite back a grin. "All right," I tell her. "Let's make it an exception."

"This entire conversation," she adds. It's not a question. "So how did it happen? How did you get... turned?"

"Lucius found me on the battlefield. I guess he saw

something in me. He was recruiting lieutenants. Turning is a difficult process. You have to drink from your sire several times. Many die or go mad. The strong survive." I shrug. "I survived."

"Your sire? And who's Lucius?"

"The owner of Club Toxic."

"Wait. Hold up." She drains her coffee, then springs up out of her chair and begins to pace back and forth in front of the huge black window. "The owner? Of Club Toxic? So there are more of you?"

Maybe opening this can of worms wasn't a good idea. As risky as it is, mind wiping is definitely easier than having this fucking conversation. "Many more. Look, Sabina—"

"No," she snaps, halting her pacing just long enough to glare at me before she resumes. "*I'm* asking the questions, Maximus."

I can't help but admire her courage. I've never seen a submissive mortal stand up to a dominant vampire this way, and while part of me longs to dispense with this tedious conversation, drag her to the bedroom, and remind her who exactly has the upper hand, the other part of me is impressed by her spirit.

"Jesus, I don't know where to start!" she mutters at length. "Where were you all day?"

"In the basement."

"In a coffin?" She sounds horrified.

I chuckle. "No. I have a vault I rest in during the daytime."

"So that myth about the sun—"

"Is no myth," I confirm. "Sunlight burns vampires to ashes."

The look she casts me then is full of something I didn't expect: pity. "So you haven't seen the sun in 1600 years?

You've never seen the stunning views from your own home?"

"No. Well, I've seen photographs."

"That's such a shame. I'm sorry."

I don't like where this is going. I cannot stand being pitied. "Don't be," I say, a little too forcefully. "I'm used to it."

I've wounded her, I can tell by the flash of hurt in her eyes before she looks away. Taking a deep breath, she composes herself for a second before she resumes her interrogation. "What about the other myths? Silver? Wooden stakes? Garlic? Oh god!" To my astonishment, she bursts out laughing and claps her hands over her mouth. "What did you think when I told you that was my safeword?"

I'm unable to stop myself from smiling back. "I must admit, I was a little surprised. I wondered whether you knew more than you were letting on."

"No. Sheer coincidence, I assure you."

"I'm actually quite partial to garlic," I tell her. "It has no ill effects. Same with silver. A stake through the heart... well, that would hurt anybody."

"I guess so." To my utter relief, she stops pacing then and turns to face me. "Maximus," she says softly.

"Yes, pet?"

"Do you think I could have another coffee?"

15

S *abina*

I SHOULD BE MORE afraid than I am but somehow even now, knowing what I know, I'm not scared of the tall, handsome man who's currently getting me another coffee from his fancy machine. If anything, I'm even more attracted to him.

And I don't know what that says about me.

My mind is still reeling from the revelations. It's too much to take in. Maximus is wearing lounge pants and a black t-shirt, and his huge biceps ripple as he opens the fridge to get the cream. I try to distract myself from the sudden surge of lust by thinking about all the things he must have seen, must have experienced. Sixteen centuries. The Dark Ages. The Middle Ages. The plague. The Renaissance. The Victorian era. Both world wars.

I can't wrap my head around it.

"Thank you," he says, setting my mug down on the counter in front of me.

"For what?"

"Not asking me to take you home yet. I like you, Sabina. And I still want to protect you."

The irony is not lost on me and I give a short bark of laughter. "From Zeke? The vampire wants to protect me from my jerk ex-boyfriend?"

His pale blue eyes flash with sudden irritation. "Watch it," he says. "I don't like being mocked."

"I'm sorry," I say, and I mean it. "I'm just... this is all so much to take in."

There's a pause, and I blow on my coffee before taking a sip.

"You have no need to fear me, pet," Maximus says, "but you should fear Zeke. Don't underestimate him."

"I don't want to talk about Zeke. I want to talk some more about you."

"I don't want to talk about myself."

We glare at each other. I look away first, taken aback by the tingles in my lower belly his expression is causing. Why do I have to want him so much?

"You should eat something," he tells me at length. "Are you sure you're not hungry?"

"Not really. You?"

He grins. "I already ate. But I could eat again."

My face grows hot as I remember the sensation of his teeth in my neck, the thumps of pleasure so intense that I actually passed out. A hot warmth shoots through my sex. "Do you even eat real food?"

"I can, but I don't have to."

I go to take another sip of coffee but realize I've already finished it.

"Sabina."

"Yes?" I almost follow that up with *Sir* but catch myself just in time. What is it about this guy? Even the discovery that he's an actual vampire hasn't made me stop wanting him.

"I need to take a quick shower. Will you still be here when I'm done?"

"You don't want me to join you?" The words have left my lips before I even thought about saying them.

He raises a dark eyebrow. "If you wish. But be warned, I'm not in a very gentle mood."

His warning only serves to make my clit ache more. "Noted."

He takes me by the hand and leads me upstairs to the bathroom attached to the room I slept in. The shower is huge, easily big enough for two people, with several fancy looking attachments.

"Strip," he says in that low, dominant tone, and my heart skips a beat. It only takes a moment to tug my dress off over my head and cast it aside.

He's staring at me now, his hungry gaze taking in every inch of my naked body. My nipples harden. Even though he's seen all of me before, I feel the heat creeping over my cheeks as the seconds tick by and he's still watching me, unblinking.

"Your turn," I say, desperate to lighten the mood.

He strips off his t-shirt and shucks off his pants, and I get to see him naked for the first time. He's just as gorgeous with his clothes off as he is in a suit. His broad chest is covered with a smattering of dark hair, and tapers down to a narrow waist and flat, ripped belly. His six pack ripples as he prowls towards me, his huge cock already jutting out.

"You're beautiful," he growls, stroking my hair back from

my face. Then he bends his head, and his lips come down on mine.

He tastes of coffee and something else, something dark and delicious. I kiss him back hungrily, running my hands over his broad shoulders as he crushes me against him, his tongue delving into my mouth as his palms cup my ass and pull me to him.

My heart is racing, I can't breathe, I don't want to breathe. I want him inside me, I want more of him, I want to kneel at his feet and worship this dark, dangerous man.

This vampire.

I push that thought away as he finally breaks the kiss, taking my hand and leading me to the shower stall.

Maximus tugs a lever, pushes a button, and then we're in the shower, the warm water raining down on us as he yanks me to him again and resumes kissing me.

Somehow, when I'm in his arms, nothing else matters. Sparks of electric lust shoot through my core at the feel of his lips on mine, and I'm unable to suppress a moan when he breaks away and begins biting his way down my neck and to my breast—careful, measured nips of my flesh hard enough to make me gasp. When he wraps his lips around my nipple and begins to suck, I clutch at his head and groan at the exquisite sensation.

"Nuh-uh," he says, releasing my taut bud long enough to speak. "Hands above your head against the wall."

The tile is cold against my skin but I obey without hesitation, marveling at the way he can fill me with trepidation and desire at the same time.

Only when he's sucked my nipple raw does he move to the other one and begin the process anew, until I'm whimpering, begging him to please, please... I don't know what I want him to do but I want this exquisite torture to stop.

At last, he gives my nipple a savage nip and releases it. "Spread your legs," he growls. "Further... that's it. Close your eyes."

I'm breathless, my heart is pounding as I do as he says and wait. The warm water is cascading over my shoulders and my clit feels huge, desperate for his touch. It wouldn't take much to finish me—I'm already so close...

I hear it a split-second before I feel it. Maximus has switched one of the shower heads to the jet setting and before I've even realized what he intends to do, he's directed it between my spread thighs, the pounding stream of water shooting directly onto my aching, pulsating nub.

The orgasm hits me almost instantly. I'm vaguely aware of him saying something but I can't make out the words, what with the roaring of the water and the sensations flooding through my every nerve ending. My thighs are shaking and I'm clenching my hands together to keep them above my head as wave after wave of pleasure courses through me before my climax finally begins to ebb. I'm over-stimulated now, and the strong jet of water is too much for my raw clit. I twist my hips, trying to get away, but Maximus claps one strong hand against my belly and pins me to the wall.

"You think you can just come without permission?" he snarls, shifting the stream closer so it's pounding me even harder.

I'm mewling, my entire world, all my focus reduced just to the intolerable stimulation on my most sensitive spot.

"This is what happens to bad little girls who come without permission," he goes on. "They get punished." His hand on my belly slides down over my pubic bone and tugs the hood back from my clit, exposing my abused button even more directly to the agony.

"Pleasepleaseplease..." I'm chanting, frantic, desperate for him to stop. "I'm sorry!" Even as I say it, I realize that the sensation has shifted again. I'm not sure whether he's redirected the stream, but the pain is morphing back into pleasure.

"Hmm," he says, and I can hear the smile in his voice. "It never ceases to amaze me what the female body is capable of." He's moving the jet now, back and forth, massaging my clit back toward yet another peak. "If you push through the pain..."

My moan is strangled, echoing off the tiled walls.

"Are you going to come again without permission, pet?"

"No! No, Sir. No, never!" I'm humping the air now but he's moving with me, offering me no surcease.

"Good." He switches the jet off abruptly and I hear him set the shower head aside. My clit is still thumping uncontrollably. "On your knees. Keep your eyes closed. Hands behind your back and open your mouth."

I've never been a big fan of giving head but suddenly I'm overwhelmed with the need to taste him and I slowly lower myself into position. For a moment he makes me wait, then I feel the big, round tip of his cock sliding against my lips.

"If you do a good job," he growls, "I might let you come again. If not..."

The threat hangs unspoken in the air but it's unnecessary. I want to please him, want to make him feel as good as he made me feel. His fingers thread through my wet hair, snagging a knot, but my gasp of pain is muffled by his thick length pressing slowly into my mouth.

"Can you take it all, little pet?"

I'm not sure but I'm certainly going to try. I relax my throat as he clutches my head and pushes his shaft deeper inside. One of my exes had a thing for blow jobs, and I'm glad for the training now as Maximus begins to fuck my throat slowly, carefully at first, my lips stretched wide around his considerable girth.

He lets out a groan and I feel it all the way down to my toes. "I'm impressed, pet," he says, letting me come up for air by pulling himself out and stroking his shaft for a moment. Opening my eyes, I see a tiny pearl of pre-cum is glistening on the tip and I'm suddenly desperate to taste it. "You have been trained well. No gag reflex at all?"

"Not if the angle's right," I say, delighted by the praise.

"Very good. Open up."

Soon, he's pumping his thick cock in and out of my mouth, clutching my head to guide me. My pussy is dripping and feels achingly empty. I wonder whether he's going to come now or still plans to fuck me. He's gotten rougher, and I'm unable to suppress the sounds I make when he hits the back of my throat, or the strands of drool which are coating my chin and dripping to my breasts.

"Gods," he groans, "I could do this all day."

My knees are aching and my toes cramping, curled as they are beneath my kneeling form, but I welcome the discomfort if it's bringing him pleasure.

"But that's enough... for now." He tugs himself out of my mouth with a wet pop and I look up at him, my eyes watering. "Let's do what we came in here to do and then take this next door."

I'm hopelessly aroused, and it's hard to concentrate on washing my hair and soaping my body with his huge frame beside me in the shower, but I manage it. He seems to be in a hurry as well, and within minutes, we're wrapped in big fluffy towels and drying ourselves off.

It seems so natural, so normal. As though it were part of a daily routine. I realize with a jolt that part of me wishes that were the case. Luckily, he distracts me from going down that trail of thought by pulling me against him and kissing me hungrily.

Nobody has ever kissed me the way he does. His lips and tongue are a revelation as they conquer my own. Every square inch of my skin tingles and I feel like I'm drowning in his taste, his scent, his proximity. When my knees are about to give way, he licks my lower lip and grins down at me. "Ready for round two?"

16

M*aximus*

I'VE HAD many women over the years but few ever affected me the way Sabina is doing. She's wide-eyed innocence one minute, hungry little slut the next, and it's the most beguiling combination.

She tastes of sunshine and honey, and smells sweeter than the most fragrant rose. When she comes, her blue eyes darken to the point where they're almost navy, and the sounds she makes go straight to my cock.

I throw her down on the bed the moment we've entered the room and she lies there, gloriously naked, gazing up at me with her big, liquid eyes. Her pretty pink cunt is still swollen from the shower and I can't decide which I want to bury inside it more: my tongue or my dick.

"Spread your legs nice and wide for me... that's it," I tell her, gratified when she obeys without hesitation. Clambering onto the bed, I lower my face until it's right above her exposed pussy and inhale deeply, my cock twitching as I catch the combined scents of her arousal and the blood rushing close to the surface of her soft skin. "What are you not going to do?" I ask her, deliberately using my firm voice.

"Come without permission," she whispers.

"Good girl." I begin to tease her, licking her inner thighs, her plump nether lips, plunging my tongue inside her tight pussy and even lapping at her crinkled little asshole—everywhere but where she wants it the most: on her straining, erect little clit. I bite the soft skin of her lower belly and lick every inch of her sex greedily, clamping my hands on her waist to hold her in place when she begins to writhe, hoping to guide my tongue to where she's most desperate to feel it.

By the time I'm ready to give her what she desires, her chest is heaving and the arousal is dripping out of her pussy and trickling down over her puckered little hole. I'm going to fuck her there, too, I've decided. I want to take her in every way there is, over and over again until I've ruined her for anybody else.

Slowly, carefully, I tug the hood back from her taut clit and wrap my lips around it, sucking gently.

"Oh god!" Sabina cries out, her hands finding my head and clutching it hard. "Please, Sir..."

"Not yet." My words are muffled but she heard them all the same, and I feel her tense. My cock is aching, my balls heavy. *Soon*, I tell myself. Just a little more torture. I do so love it when she begs.

I push Sabina to the brink and keep her there, alternately sucking and licking her hard little bud until she's incoherent and my chin is drenched. Only then do I rear up and position myself on top of her, the tip of my cock teasing her entrance.

"Wait," she whispers, "do we have a condom?"

Drat. I hate those things. Now would not be a good time to tell her I can't actually get her pregnant. "No," I say, and begin to pull away but she clutches at me.

"It's okay," she says. "Please. I want to feel you... all of you."

For a brief second I wonder what's come over me, this kind of reckless behavior isn't like me at all, but then I'm sliding inside her tight, wet heat and everything else fades into the background. Gods, she feels even better than I had imagined. I'm not going to last long, and I want to make her scream again before I'm done.

Rearing up, I wrap a hand around her slender, pale throat and change the angle of my pelvis so I'm grinding against her sensitive button with each thrust. Her reaction is instant. "Please," she begs in a strangled voice, "please let me come."

I increase the pace, careful to keep my grip on her throat gentle enough to let her breathe. She's so slippery and yet I can feel the walls of her pussy begin to flutter as I fuck her with all the hunger and passion inside me.

"With me," I growl, and allow myself to lose what little hold I had remaining over my control. I'm slamming into her with all my might, feeling the pleasure building, building—until I go over the edge with a roar.

I come so hard I see stars, and I'm vaguely aware that she's coming too, her cunt contracting rhythmically around my jerking cock.

Her cries are music to my ears.

Only after we're both spent do I let go of her throat and

slump over her, careful to keep most of my weight on my arm so as not to crush her.

"Oh wow," she murmurs, and I can hear the smile in her voice. "That was amazing."

My face is buried in the crook of her neck but I'm grinning too. "And I didn't even bite you."

She lets out a delighted-sounding giggle. "Surely you wouldn't do that every time. I don't think I'd survive it!"

"No, I don't think you would." With a sigh, I ease myself out of her, astonished at the flood of our combined juices that spills onto the sheets. "We made quite a mess."

"I have an IUD," she says, "and I never usually have unprotected sex. I just wanted to feel you. It's not like me at all..."

"It's okay," I tell her. "It's the same for me." I'm suddenly exhausted, overcome with the need to close my eyes for a few moments. "Pet?"

"Yes, Sir?"

I pull her into my arms until she's resting her head on my chest. Her cheek is hot against my skin. "Can we just lie here quietly for a few? I need to recover. After all, I am quite an old man."

She lets out another delightful giggle. "Of course, Sir."

"Then we'll clean up and go back to your place, check on Felix. Get you some food."

"All right."

My eyes are closed but even as I doze, I'm aware of everything: her scent, the feel of her, the warmth of her satiny skin against mine. Her hair, still damp from the shower, is trailing over my chest.

A little thought floats unbidden into my mind, searing its way into my consciousness before I can suppress it: I never want to let her go.

Sabina

I'VE NEVER DONE DRUGS, aside from the requisite few tugs on a joint in my late teens, but this is how I always imagined it would feel: insanely good, even though you know it's bad for you. I can't put my finger on what it is about Maximus that makes me feel so very drawn to him, but I'm helpless to fight it.

For god's sake, the man is a vampire, and instead of doing what any sensible woman would do—run a mile—I jumped back into bed with him.

This is taking masochism too far.

Even so, as I lie with my head resting on his huge shoulder, examining every angle of his striking face, I don't regret staying. He may not be husband—hell, probably not even boyfriend—material but it's the best sex I've ever had, and I'm not about to give that up anytime soon. Call it insane chemistry or even just naked lust, but I'm riding this train until I'm forced to disembark.

I should write Zeke a thank you letter. Had he not sent me those threatening texts, I may never have seen Maximus again. Or had I not met Ethan. Funny how two such jerks led me to this amazing man.

Life is strange sometimes.

Maximus looks less fearsome with his eyes closed, his long, dark lashes stark against his pale skin. His wide, generous mouth is slightly parted, and a shiver runs through me at the memory of what he can do with those lips. That tongue.

Even though my pussy is raw and aching, still sticky from before, it pulses when I think about how he licked me earlier, and I force my thoughts to return to the present. Maximus may be exhausted enough to nap but I'm wide awake and alert, still trying to process the events of the past couple of days.

Is Club Toxic really full of vampires? Are there female vampires too, or are they all men? Did Zeke somehow know it; was that why he warned me to stay away? Was he really trying to protect rather than threaten me?

Oh god, now that Maximus has bitten me, am *I* a vampire?

I lie there for a long while, tormented by questions, and am beyond relieved when he opens his eyes, interrupting my ruminations.

"You didn't sleep?" he says in a throaty voice.

"No."

"Are you all right? You look pale."

"Am I a vampire now?" I blurt out the fear which has been consuming me ever since the idea first entered my head.

He lets out a chuckle of genuine amusement. "No, pet. It's not that easy to turn someone."

"Oh. Good."

"Good?" He turns to look at me and raises a dark eyebrow. "You wouldn't want to be a vampire?" He sounds faintly insulted.

"No! I mean... I hadn't even thought about... I mean, I don't know enough—"

Maximus interrupts my babbling with another chuckle. "I'm just messing with you."

"Oh." *Bastard*. My tummy takes that moment to growl loudly in the silence.

"We should get you fed," he says, dropping a kiss on the top of my head and shifting me off him.

"Could I have another quick shower first?"

"Certainly. I won't join you this time, otherwise we'll end up back here. I'll go down to the kitchen and find you something to eat."

"All right." Part of me is disappointed we won't be having sex again but when I move to get out of bed, my sore muscles protest and I realize it might be better to give my body a little break.

I don't wash my hair again, instead I just lather and rinse my armpits and between my legs. My dress is still on the bathroom floor where I left it, and even though I'm loath to put it back on, I don't have any other options. It will be good to get home so I can change.

When I enter the kitchen, Maximus is sliding a couple of toasted sandwiches onto a plate. "I hope you like cheese and tomato," he says, pushing the plate towards me.

"I do."

"I'd give it a moment, they're probably hot."

"Thank you." The glass of water he sets in front of me is welcome and I take a huge gulp.

"Will you be all right here for a few minutes? I thought I'd shower and clean up myself up while you eat," he says.

"Sure."

"Your phone should be charged by now, too."

"Thank you," I say again. "Um... Sir?"

"Yes, pet?"

"Do you have anything for me to wear?" I indicate my rumpled dress. "Anything more comfortable?"

He grins, and I realize for the first time that he has a tiny dimple in his left cheek. "I'll see if I can find something. Back in a few."

I watch his broad, naked back disappear through the doorway and take a bite of my sandwich. It's delicious, and I realize just how hungry I really was. Before I've even realized it, I've eaten both toasties and drained my water. After taking the plate and my glass to the enormous double sink, I go to where my phone is charging and pluck it from the pad.

I have a couple of messages—one from my sister, asking why I haven't called her back yet, and one from Zeke.

You can't hide from me forever.

What the hell is this guy's deal? I'm more angry than afraid. Regardless of what Maximus says, I know Zeke, and his bark is way worse than his bite. Still, it's better if Maximus doesn't see that latest message. It will only fire up his weird overprotective streak again. Clicking the screen off, I shove my phone into my bag.

"These are probably a bit big for you but they should do for long enough until we get to your place," Maximus says, tossing a bundle of clothing my way.

It's a dark blue t-shirt and a black pair of sweatpants. "Thank you," I say, stripping off my dress and pulling the t-shirt over my head. It feels good to be wearing something clean.

Maximus is watching me as I get changed, and the dark hunger in his eyes makes my lower belly clench. Will I ever not want him? The sweatpants are far too big but they have a drawstring so I can cinch them around my waist.

"Gorgeous," he says. It's then that I realize he's wearing a suit.

"Are you... going to work?"

"After I've taken you home."

"Oh." It's all I can think of to say. The wave of disappointment I feel is as overwhelming as it is ridiculous. To hide it, I indicate my bare feet. "I can't remember where my shoes are."

"Probably upstairs. I'll go get them." He can move insanely fast when it suits him, and once again I'm left alone in the kitchen, staring at my little bag on the marble counter. So this is it then. He'll take me home and go on to the club. It's just as well, I tell myself. I have to work tomorrow, and I'll be no good to anyone if I spend all night with him. Even though I slept for the better part of the day, I'll need to get at least some rest if I want to keep my job.

"Here you go." Maximus has reappeared as quickly as he had gone, and he sets my sandals at my feet. I put them on and lay my dress over my arm. "Ready to leave?"

"Sure." Before I follow him into the garage, I glance around the kitchen one last time, wondering whether I'll ever see it again. Somehow, I doubt it.

"Oh, did you get your phone?"

"Yes, thanks."

I wait for him to ask me if there were any messages but he remains silent, leading me into the garage and opening the passenger side door for me before getting into the driver's seat himself.

The atmosphere between us has changed slightly. I can't put my finger on how, or why, but there's a lump in my throat I can't deny as he pushes the remote to open the garage door and we head out into the Arizona night.

17

M *aximus*

SABINA IS ESSENTIALLY silent for the duration of the drive, gazing out the window and chewing her bottom lip. I'm tempted to reach into her mind to see what she's thinking but that would be taking unfair advantage. Sometimes, not using one's special powers is more difficult than using them.

Once we've reached Club Toxic, I park and get out with her, walking her to her car without being asked. "I think Felix will be pleased to see you," I say, trying to make conversation.

"I'm sure he will."

She looks adorable in my clothes, even with her makeup smudged and that sulky expression on her face. "Are you going to come into the club?" I ask.

Turning to face me, she gives me a long, measured look, then indicates what she's wearing. "Like this?"

"No, but we could make a quick stop at your place, you could get changed—"

"I have to work tomorrow. I need to get at least a couple of hours' sleep before the morning."

"It's still early. You could visit the club and still get some shuteye." I wonder why I'm so desperate to keep her with me. Why not just let her go home? As much as I want to lie to myself and say it's purely because I'm worried about her safety, I know there's more to it. I enjoy her too much. I don't want to leave her side.

"No, thank you," she says stiffly. "I'm not really in a clubbing mood. And I should spend at least some time with my cat before leaving him again."

"Have you received any more text messages?" I finally ask the question which has been eating at me ever since she retrieved her freshly charged phone.

A tiny pause. Then, "No."

I know she's lying. But she's a grown woman, and even though we've played, she's not officially mine. At this point, there's nothing I can do. Gods, but I hate feeling helpless. "Promise me you would tell me if you did? I worry about you, Sabina."

"You don't need to worry. I can take care of myself."

She's as infuriating as she is pretty. "Pet, I don't know what I've done to upset you, but please let's talk about this." I hate feeling like I'm begging but I don't want us to part this way. If I can't spend more time with her tonight, I want to see her again as soon as possible.

"You've done nothing to upset me," she says. Lying again. "I'm just tired."

"What are you doing tomorrow after work? I just realized I don't even know what you do."

"A veterinarian's assistant," she says curtly. "And I don't know. I don't have any plans."

"I could pick you up. We could do something."

"I'll think about it."

"Give me your phone." I use my dominant tone and she flinches.

"Why?"

"Unlock it and give it to me. I want to give you my number."

"I can put it in myself." She fishes her cell out of her little bag and taps the screen a few times. "Go on."

I'm fully aware that she's doing this on purpose, that she doesn't want me to have the phone because she's received another message, but at this point I don't know what else to do about it. I give her my number and pray that she's putting it in correctly.

"Thanks," she says, fishing out her keys and sliding her phone back into her purse. "I'll let you know."

Unable to stop myself, I grab her shoulders and crush her lips with my own, kissing her greedily. She's rigid for a second but then relaxes into my arms, her mouth opening, yielding to my tongue. Her little nipples harden against my chest, poking against my sweatshirt, and I catch a whiff of fresh arousal. When she lets out a moan, I wrench myself away.

"Drive safely," I tell her. "Do me one favor and text me when you get home."

"Why?" Her eyes have gone dark with desire but now they're wide with suspicion.

"So I know you're safe." And so I have her phone number.

She lets out a little snort. "You don't think I'm capable of driving home?"

Gods but I want to shake her sometimes. "That's not what I said. I just... look, I'm still worried about your ex lurking around. Like I said, I know his type. Please just do that for me. One little message."

Sabina rolls her eyes. "All right. Anyone ever tell you you're overprotective?"

I flash her my most disarming grin. "All the time."

She turns to get into her car, reaches to open the door, and I resist the urge to give her round ass a quick slap. Once she's seated in her shabby old Explorer, she rolls the window down. "Have a good evening," she says.

"You too. And think of me when you go to bed. No coming without permission."

A flicker of something I can't identify flashes across her eyes but it's gone in an instant. "Good night, Maximus." Without waiting for a response, she fires up the engine and pulls away from the curb.

I watch her car until the taillights have disappeared, a sinking feeling in my gut. I don't know where she lives. I don't have her phone number. I don't even know her last name.

I don't care about my clothes, they're easily replaced. But she holds all the cards now. If she decides she never wants to see me again, I'll never be able to find her, and I can't stand that thought.

How did I allow that to happen? I'm used to being the one in control, both in and out of the bedroom. It's like my ability to think rationally flies out of the window when I'm around her.

Suppressing a sigh, rubbing the back of my head, I make my way toward the entrance to the club. There's the usual line of people waiting to get in and I prowl right past them, barely acknowledging my colleagues at the door.

My phone is burning a hole in my pocket as I wait for Sabina's text. How long does it take to drive from here to her place? Did she ever say?

I should have jumped back in my car and followed her home.

But as I said: rational thought. Reason. Gone.

Several people greet me as I head down the stairs to the lower level but I only mutter curtly in reply. My thoughts are with a tall, blue-eyed girl with a Roman name and the sweetest blood I've tasted in a century.

"Maximus!" A flushed, willow-thin brunette grabs my arm.

I blink and slowly her face swims into focus. Gods but I'm distracted. That is not good. "Leann, what can I do for you?"

She's a regular at Toxic, a sweetblood who's addicted to playing with—and being sipped on by—vampires. I've enjoyed her myself more than once. "Do you know that guy over there?" Leann indicates a man standing in the shadows close to the bar. He's wearing a dark suit and it's impossible to guess his age from this distance.

"Can't say I do," I say honestly. "Never seen him before."

"He's a vampire though, right?"

"He is." We can always sense our own kind.

"Well, I've agreed to play with him. Will you please look out for me?"

"Out here or in a booth?"

"Over there." She points to the farthest public play area from us; a spanking bench with restraints.

"Of course," I tell her. "Just let me know when you're about to start. Come find me."

"Thank you. It shouldn't be long." She turns and strides back to the man in question, her scarlet, skintight dress emphasizing her narrow hips. I can't help but compare her boyish ass to Sabina's plumper, rounder one.

Get a grip on yourself, Maximus. You have a job to do.

My phone vibrates in my pocket and I snatch it out, flicking it on to see a text from Sabina: *I'm home safely, Sir.*

Grinning, beyond relieved to at least now have her number, I text back two simple words.

Good girl.

~

Sabina

It's been a long day and the sun is only now beginning to set.

Last night, after I got home, I made myself something to eat, took a hot bath, and played with Felix before dropping into bed, exhausted.

But before doing any of those things, I texted Maximus. It was against my better judgment but the reward—his reply —was instant.

Good girl.

Funny how two little words can have such an effect on a girl. On me, anyway.

When at last I dropped into sleep, I dreamed of him. I woke up wet and aching, but there was no time to do anything about it as I had to hurry to get ready for work. I don't know whether I would have otherwise. He told me not to, and I seem to be obeying his orders for reasons I don't quite understand.

I was distracted all day at work, my mind constantly on the tall, dark, handsome dom who makes my knees buckle when he kisses me. He did that intentionally last night, before letting me go outside the club—giving me a reminder of just how easily he can make me melt.

On my lunch break, I saw he'd texted me: *I want to see you again tonight. Let me come over.* My body reacted instantly to the thought of seeing him again, of feeling his touch, so like a drug. With my heart hammering against my ribs, I replied, telling him yes and giving him my address.

Only now, as I pace back and forth in my den, watching the sky slowly darken, am I second-guessing my decision.

I didn't want it to seem like I'd made too much of an effort, so I'm wearing black yoga pants and a pale blue halter top. My nipples are already stabbing against the cotton. I showered, shaved, blow-dried my hair and put on some makeup—but not as much as I would if I were going to the club. I don't know whether he's on duty tonight. He made no mention of it. And even though I've been thinking about it all afternoon, I haven't decided whether I'd accompany him if he were.

It's not just because I have to get up early for work and can't be gallivanting around until the early hours on a weeknight. It's because of what he said about Toxic being full of vampires. The owner being a vampire. What had Maximus called him? Lucius. The sire.

Sometimes I still wonder whether I'm just dreaming all this.

Despite Maximus's fears, I haven't heard another word from Zeke. I'm refusing to respond to him so he's probably gotten bored. Thank god. Him continuing to harass me would be a complication I don't need.

Realizing that Maximus won't be getting here for quite some time, as he likely doesn't even awaken before dark, I go to my little kitchen and open a bottle of Merlot. Pouring myself a large glass, I take it to the sofa and curl up.

Felix jumps up to join me, his purring like the distant rumble of thunder. I scratch between his ears with my free hand as he lies down beside me.

My phone rings. It's still on the kitchen counter, where I left it, and I curse as I scramble to get to it in time. My sister's name is flashing up on the screen and I realize I had promised to call her.

Crap.

Feeling guilty, I slide the button to answer. "Hey Lissy," I say.

"Are you avoiding me?"

"No! No, I promise. Sorry, I've just been busy."

"You live alone. No kids. No man. You only work until five. How busy can you be?"

I roll my eyes. Sometimes she behaves more like my older sister than my little one. "You'd be surprised," I say drily.

"I wanted to ask whether you're free for dinner tomorrow night. I'm having a few people over. You dumped that Zeke guy, right?"

I don't like where this is going. This is not the first time she's tried to set me up with someone under the guise of inviting me to dinner. It's always a complete disaster. Either she's trying to find me a man, or she needs to borrow money. Sometimes it's both. "Yes, but—"

"Great, then I'll see you tomorrow. Eight sharp."

"Lissy, I haven't—"

I stare at the phone. She hung up on me. I'm tempted to call her back and give her a piece of my mind but there's no point. She's wild, reckless, everything I'm not. She jumps from man to man, has a huge and unpredictable, colorful circle of friends, and is constantly getting herself into situations she needs rescuing from.

I'm just the idiot who cleans up her messes. It's been that way ever since we were small. Part of me resents it. I'm the eldest, so I've always felt responsible. And it was fine when we were kids with no parents. But now she's thirty. Surely that's old enough to start taking care of herself?

I've just slumped back onto the couch when my doorbell makes me start.

Maximus.

Felix, always curious about visitors, trots along by my feet as I go to open the door. Sometimes he behaves more like a dog than a cat.

Maximus is standing there clutching a bunch of flowers, sinfully gorgeous in his usual suit. His intent gaze takes in my yoga pants and top and he raises a dark eyebrow. "Are we staying in?" he says by way of greeting.

"We didn't discuss specific plans. I can always get changed," I say defensively. "Are those for me?"

"Yes." He hands me the bouquet.

"Thank you. Please come in." As he steps over the threshold, I look down to find Felix so I can introduce them, but he's vanished. "Would you like anything to drink? Coffee? Tea? Wine? I might still have a beer in the fridge. I just need to put these in some water." I'm babbling, suddenly filled with nerves, unsettled by the way his proximity turns my core liquid.

"I'd love some wine but I'm driving. Unless you'd like me to stay the night?"

I freeze with my hand on the fridge door handle. "Don't you have to work?"

He lets out a dark chuckle. "I do. I just wanted to see how you'd react."

I don't like being toyed with. Grimly, I get a pair of scissors and set about trimming the stalks of the flowers he got me. I've never had a green thumb and couldn't name them to save my life, but they're pink and pretty. I wonder whether I have a suitable vase somewhere. I don't ever get given flowers. "Well, now you know," I manage.

"I thought you said you have a cat?"

"I do. He's around here somewhere." If I had any remaining doubt that Maximus isn't quite human, Felix's reaction has removed it. He always greets visitors, sniffing their shoes. "He's shy," I lie.

I thought Maximus had gone and sat down in the den but then his hands land on my shoulders from behind and I almost jump out of my skin.

"Hush," he says quietly, "I just wanted to say hello properly. Put the scissors down and turn to face me."

When he uses that tone, I'm helpless to resist. It's almost like I'm hypnotized. I do as he says.

"You look beautiful," he murmurs, then his lips land on mine.

Immediately, I'm drowning, clinging to him, my skin prickling and my core pulsing with need. I forget to think, to breathe... all that exists in the world is this man and how he's making me feel.

His hand slides down my back to cup my buttock and he tugs me close so I can feel the thick, hard length of him through his suit pants. He pulls his face back just far enough to growl, "Were you a good girl, pet? Or did you masturbate since I saw you last?"

"No." My voice is a croak. "I was good, Sir."

"Then you deserve a reward." Before I realize what's happening, he's stripped off my pants and panties, freed his erection, picked me up and impaled me with his huge cock.

The sound I make is inhuman but I can't help it. His kiss alone has me so slippery that he slides in easily, stretching me to the point of exquisite pain.

Perching me on the counter, he nuzzles my neck and I throw my head back, lost in the sensation of his gently rocking hips against my core. "I've been thinking about doing this all day," he mumbles against my skin, and I feel the nip of his teeth. "I'm so hungry for you, Sabina."

My nails are digging into his suit jacket and I wrap my legs around his waist, desperate for him to go deeper. Harder. Faster. I'm already so close.

"You're going to come around my cock like a good little pet," he tells me, upping the pace of his thrusts enough to make me moan helplessly. "Aren't you?"

"Yes, Sir." He shifts the angle of his pelvis, crushing my pounding clit with each deep stroke. "Oh god, please..."

"Now," he growls, and my orgasm crashes over me like a tsunami. I'm drowning in pleasure, clutching him as if he were a life raft as wave after wave of hot, liquid pleasure radiates through my entire body.

Then there's a sharp stinging pain in my neck, and everything goes dark...

18

M aximus

IT'S BEEN NEARLY a week since a certain blonde entered my world, and I can no longer imagine my life without her in it —a thought which terrifies me.

We haven't been able to see as much of each other as we'd like, what with her working during the day and me at night, but every moment I spend with her makes me want more, regardless of whether we're playing, fucking, or just talking. She's bright and witty, and a delight to behold in the throes of both pain and pleasure.

Unfortunately, she's also as stubborn as a mule, and while she trusts me completely with her body, she's very guarded with details about her feelings, her past, her thoughts. For instance, I know Zeke is still threatening her, but she hasn't mentioned it since that first night she spent at my house. And every time I try to broach the topic, she changes the subject or distracts me in other, physical ways.

It's infuriating.

She's fast asleep now, naked in my arms, and I decide to give her another few minutes before rousing her. I took the night off so we could spend it together. She came to my place shortly after sunset. I ordered pizza and we watched a movie. Then I tormented her beautiful naked body with ice cubes and hot wax before fucking her into oblivion.

Sabina always passes out when I feed from her. I noticed that when I first went to her condo and took her on the kitchen counter. She's never under for long, though, and the look she gives me when she comes to—so open and trusting —slays me. I could drown in her eyes.

She got changed and came to the club with me that night, although we didn't play. She stayed by my side and sipped a glass of wine, watching others indulge in public sessions, allowing me to introduce her to some of my colleagues. Lucius and Selene were in that evening, sitting tall and grand on their thrones, and I debated for a moment whether to introduce her to them, too, but decided it was too soon.

Even though I haven't felt this way about anybody since Caroline, I have no way of knowing how Sabina feels about me. She enjoys what I do to her, there's no doubt about that, but we've talked about the past as little as we've talked about the future. Her past, anyway. Ever since she learned the truth about me, she's enjoyed badgering me with questions about certain periods in history which interest her. And I'm happy to answer what I can. I admire that she always wants to learn more. Know more.

I just wish she were more forthcoming about herself.

Her eyes flutter open and she turns to look at me. "Maximus," she sighs, and the way she says my name goes right through me.

"Pet."

"Was I asleep long?"

"No. I was about to wake you."

She moves and lets out a little moan. "For round two?"

"You're insatiable." I kiss the top of her head.

"Only with you." Her full lips curve into a satisfied smile. "I can never get enough of what you do to me."

"The feeling's mutual."

Her hand slides down to find my cock but I catch it and move it away.

"I want to talk," I tell her.

She stiffens, the sudden tension radiating off her. "That sentence never leads to anything good."

"Nothing bad. I just... all this time we're spending together, and I still know next to nothing about you."

"There's nothing to know." Her face has taken on that familiar, shuttered look.

"I don't believe that. You've been hurt."

She lets out a little huff. "Everyone's been hurt."

"That's true." In my experience, people are more willing to open up if you lead by example. I swallow and close my eyes, praying that I won't regret what I'm about to do. "I've been hurt."

"By whom?" She's watching me intently now.

"Caroline."

"Your lover?"

"My wife."

There's a long pause, and I realize I would give anything to know what Sabina is thinking right now. But I resist the temptation to peek into her mind. If she's jealous, she's not showing it.

"What did she do?"

"She did nothing. The fault was mine."

"All right. What did *you* do?"

"I failed to protect her. She had a little shop. She made hats. I allowed it—she enjoyed it and was good—"

"You *allowed* it?" Sabina echoes with disbelief in her voice. "How generous of you! When was this, exactly?"

Ignoring the barb, I continue. "1895. Not all married women were permitted to work. But as I was saying, she was good at it and enjoyed it. People came from all over to buy her adornments."

"And what did you do? What was your trade?"

"I bought and sold horses."

"I suppose they were more popular back then," she says with a smile.

I suppress a huff of irritation. "Regardless, Caroline was working late. She had an express assignment she wanted to finish. I was supposed to go and pick her up, to escort her from the shop back to our house. I never let her go out on her own after dark. But I overslept." I realize I'm clenching my fists and force myself to unclench them. The memory is still as raw and painful as it was a century ago. "I don't know whether she was just unwilling to wait, or whether she thought I wasn't coming, but she set off alone. On foot. In the heart of London. She disobeyed me." I pause, working up the nerve to continue.

"What happened?" Sabina's voice is barely above a whisper. She's squeezing my thigh gently.

"She was set upon by a group of men. They... raped her and plunged a knife into her heart before stealing her jewels. They were drunk, the police said, they got carried away. They were caught and hanged, but of course that didn't bring her back." *You should have turned her.* It's a sentence which has haunted me ever since, but I don't speak it aloud. I look down to see a tear sliding down Sabina's cheek.

"I'm so sorry, Maximus."

"I should have been there. I should never have let her go out alone. I was her *husband*! It was my job to protect her."

"It wasn't your fault! Surely you don't blame yourself?"

"Of course I do!" My tone is more forceful than I had intended and I wince. "Sorry. It's hard for me to talk about."

"Is that why you work security now? Why you're so protective? Why you freaked out about those messages from Zeke?"

"Partly. I vowed two things on the day we buried her. That I would spend the rest of eternity looking out for others, and—" I stop, suddenly realizing what I'm about to say.

"And?" she probes.

"It doesn't matter."

She lets out a little sigh. "I can guess."

"Really?"

"It's not hard. You vowed never to love again, didn't you?"

I swallow past the lump in my throat, unwilling to admit it but unwilling to lie to her.

"It doesn't matter," she says, turning her head and kissing my chest. "What matters is that you still blame yourself after all this time when you shouldn't. Stuff happens. Bad things happen."

That a girl who's only been alive for three and a half decades should be explaining the realities of the world to me is somehow adorable, and I find myself smiling despite the raw pain the memory has evoked. "I know, pet," I say at length. "But I intend to make sure fewer bad things happen. And I like to think I've saved some people since that day."

"I'm sure you've saved more than you know."

There's a pause, and I can almost feel Sabina wrestling with herself. I wait, knowing that silence is often the best way to get someone to keep talking. She doesn't disappoint me.

"Zeke has messaged me again. Twice."

A surge of anger rises up in my chest and I force myself to keep my tone even. "Thank you for telling me. But you haven't seen him?"

"No. I honestly believe he's just trying to intimidate me. Although I have no idea why."

I could tell her but I won't. "Will you show me the messages?" I say instead.

"My phone is downstairs."

"Later then."

She's biting her bottom lip, and I wonder whether it's because she's annoyed with herself for telling me, or worried about how I'll react to the messages when I see them. After a moment, she sighs. "All right."

"Good girl."

"Maximus?"

"Yes, pet?"

"Thank you for telling me about Caroline. I feel like I know you a little better now."

"Good. Do you think someday you'll return the favor?"

"How?"

"By telling me something about you. From your past. Sharing one's pain often helps ease it."

"I don't like to talk about myself." Her face is closed off again. "I never have."

I know better than to push it. Instead, I pull her closer and drop another kiss on the top of her head. "Well," I tell her, "if you ever change your mind, I'd love to know more about you. I want to know everything about you."

"If I ever change my mind, I promise you'll be the first to find out."

Not for the first time, I wonder what exactly has wounded my little pet so badly that she's so unwilling to talk about it. One day, I *will* find out.

❧

Sabina

As much as I enjoy spending time with Maximus, I wish he'd stop probing me about my past. I don't see how his knowing more about my childhood will change anything. Besides, it's not like we have any kind of future together. He's a *vampire*. Could I really spend the rest of my life with a man who can never see the light of day?

Caroline did, a little voice in my head tells me. It was fascinating to hear Maximus tell me about her. There was a tenderness in his voice that made me feel a pang of jealousy —which is ridiculous, considering the woman died over a hundred years ago. Although it's not really her I'm jealous of. Is it the thought that he loved her as he's sworn never to love again?

"Are you thirsty?" Maximus's voice breaks into my confused thoughts.

"I could do with some coffee."

"I'll go and get you some."

I watch him as he gets out of bed and heads to the door. His back ripples with muscle, his buttocks are round and tight above thick, strong thighs. He's completely unabashed about being in the nude. Then again, he has no reason to be shy. Not with that body.

I lie back on the pillows, crossing my arms behind my head. My skin is still tingling from the sensation play we did earlier, and the throbbing sting in my neck is becoming strangely familiar. I wonder whether there are any addictive qualities in that pleasure serum vampires apparently inject when they feed. It certainly seems so. It hasn't even been a week, and already I can't bear the thought of never feeling that sensation again.

I push that line of thinking to the back of my mind. I need to figure out exactly what it is I want from this man— no, this *vampire*. Yes, he makes me laugh, yes, he makes me wet, yes, he makes me want to throw myself on my knees and serve him. He's handsome, he can be as fierce as he can be gentle, and he's loyal and protective to the core. But he says he won't ever love again. He won't ever grow older, and could potentially live forever. Would I want that? To age beside him, to watch as the wrinkles appear on my body and parts of me begin to sag while he remains the same? People would wonder what he sees in the old hag on his arm. Was Caroline willing to do that? Was Maximus so in love with her that he wouldn't have cared, would have still desired her if she'd lived to be twice his age, at least physically? And what if we had children? They would only be half-human, who knows what restrictions they would have to endure, not to mention having a father who would one day look the same age, and then younger than they.

At least hearing about what happened with his wife explains Maximus's extreme behavior when it comes to Zeke. I feel a pang of guilt when I think about how I just lied to him. Yes, Zeke has sent two more messages, but I believe he's also started skulking around the clinic where I work.

I'm almost certain I saw him duck around the corner when I left yesterday. Maybe I should tell Maximus but he'd overreact. He always does. I still don't believe Zeke would ever really harm me. Why should he? What would he gain? Whereas Maximus... I wouldn't put it past him to actually kill Zeke, should he believe it to be justified. And I don't want to risk that.

I shake my head slightly. It's all too much. Too complicated. Those are just some of the reasons why this—whatever we have between us—will never be more than an affair. Can never be more than that. Regardless of the way my heart skips a beat whenever I'm about to see Maximus. It doesn't matter how my belly clenches when he smiles at me, or my skin tingles when he touches me.

Besides, I know better than to fall in love with a man who doesn't love me back.

"Here you go, pet." Maximus has returned with a steaming mug, which he sets on the bedside table.

I struggle into an upright sitting position and take it, the delicious aroma of coffee already tickling my nose. "Thank you, Sir."

He glances at the window, even though there's nothing to see there but black glass. "We'll have our coffee, get dressed, and then I'd better take you home."

"Do you have to?" I blurt out. "It's the weekend."

He takes a sip from his own mug and raises an eyebrow. "Do you want to spend the entire day here, by yourself?"

I shrug as casually as I'm able. Does he really not realize how luxurious this house is compared to my little condo? He has not one but *three* swimming pools. Two hot tubs. Views you could lose yourself in from all windows and several outdoor decks. A huge library. A home cinema with more movies than you could count. "Do you think I'd be bored?"

He chuckles. "No, pet, I suppose not." Setting his mug aside, he draws me into his arms. "You never told me where you went on Tuesday evening. Why I couldn't see you."

Crap. I was hoping he'd forgotten. "My little sister was having a dinner party. She asked me to come."

"You could have invited me."

I'm shocked by the faint note of hurt in his tone. I want to tell him that we'd only just met and the thought hadn't even crossed my mind but I don't want to offend him further. Instead, I say, "You don't know Lissy. She always invites and cooks for a specific number of people, and doesn't take kindly to surprises."

"Were there other men there?"

Jesus. I know where this is going. "Yes." It comes out as more of a sigh. While I found his possessiveness cute at first, it's sometimes a little annoying as well. I feel like he doesn't trust me. "But none of them interested me."

"Good." He nuzzles my shoulder. "I'd like to meet Lissy someday. And... you said you had a brother?"

"Ben."

"Older, or younger?"

"He's younger too. They both are."

"Does he live here in Tucson as well?"

"No." Thank god. Being there for Lissy is hard enough, I couldn't still look out for Ben, too. "He's in Texas. He met a girl there while he was at college, and married her. They have two kids."

There is a long, long pause and for a moment, I wonder whether Maximus has fallen asleep after all. Then, "Do you think you might want kids someday?"

I stare straight ahead, wondering how loaded that question was. "I don't know. I think I always assumed I would have at least one. But I never met the right guy yet."

"Vampires can't father children," Maximus says quietly. "I believe that's something you should be made aware of."

My mind is racing as I absorb this information. "Thank you." I don't know what else to say. What else can I say? "I'm sorry."

"Don't be. It's probably for the best. We don't know what they'd be like. What their lives would be like. Can you imagine an entire childhood spent in darkness?"

I can't even imagine a month of it as an adult, but I just shake my head instead of saying so. "Awful."

There's a pause, and I get the feeling he wants to say something else but is wrestling with himself as to whether or not he should. Apparently he decides against it, because instead of speaking, he removes the now empty coffee mug from my hands, sets it down on the nightstand, and presses his lips against mine. "If we hurry," he growls once we've come up for air, "we can go for another round before bedtime." His hand trails down my belly and cups my pussy. I shudder at the sparks of lust which shoot through my core, and my thighs part automatically.

"I'd be down for that, Sir," I whisper.

"I wasn't asking."

19

M aximus

I SLEPT LIKE SHIT TODAY. I don't usually dream while I spend the daylight hours holed up in my vault, but this time I was plagued by nightmares—visions of Caroline being beaten, raped...

Even after all this time, the pain is almost visceral.

Sabina and I are at the club now. It being Saturday night, I'm on duty, but my thoughts are elsewhere. Before we left, she finally showed me the last two text messages that dirty shifter scumbag sent her. The first was essentially more of the same—a warning to stay away from Club Toxic, and reminding her that she's being watched, that she can't hide. The second, though...

If I see you with that leech again, you'll regret it.

Sabina had no idea Zeke was referring to me. How could she? And how could I explain it to her without telling her that her ex-boyfriend is a shifter? I asked her what she thought he meant and she shrugged, saying he liked to get high sometimes. Figures. A shifter and a druggie. I'm surprised he managed to hold on to her for as long as he did. Then again, she did say they only saw each other a couple of times a week.

I wish she'd take the threat more seriously but every time I mention it, she spouts the same irritating line: that she can take care of herself.

Caroline used to say the same thing whenever I lamented that I couldn't be with her during the day.

Right now, Sabina is over by the public play areas, watching an intense scene unfold with shining eyes. I'm perched on my usual stool beside the booths but I keep glancing over in her direction, partly to keep an eye on her, partly because the dim red light is making her golden hair glow sunset orange. She's wearing a short, ruffled skirt and a cropped top which leaves her midriff bare. Knee-high boots make her legs appear endless and I close my eyes against the sudden image of them wrapped around my waist as I fuck her up against the wall, right here, claiming her as mine for all to see.

When I open them again, my gaze is still directed at the scene Sabina is watching with such fascination. As Mistress Elvira slides another needle into her slave's flesh, Sabina licks her pink lips and my cock twitches. I mentally add needles to the list of things I want to do to my little pet.

"Maximus!" Leann is standing in front of me, disheveled, wringing her hands, tears streaking down her cheeks. "Didn't you hear me?"

I'm off my stool in an instant. "What happened?"

"I was screaming for you!" She lets out a half-hiccup, half-sob. "We were playing but he ignored my safeword.

Soon after we started, I felt uncomfortable and changed my mind. I asked him to stop but he—"

"Who?" I interrupt her.

"He's leaving. That one over there!" She points, and I realize her whole arm is trembling.

Fuck.

"Tiberius is at the bar," I tell her urgently, gesturing to where my friend is standing. "Go and tell him what happened. Say I sent you, and that he's to look after you until I get back. I'm going to deal with that asshole."

The moment I've finished speaking, I'm off, blurring between the club attendees, my entire focus narrowed on the back of the guy Leann pointed out. He's walking swiftly toward the stairs, a touch too fast for someone who's innocent but not fast enough to appear immediately guilty. He seems familiar, but it isn't until I reach him and halt his progress with a hand on his shoulder that I realize who he is.

"Hello Ethan," I snarl. "Didn't I warn you never to set foot in here again?"

He spins to face me and his eyes flash first with recognition, then loathing. "It's a free country," he rasps.

"Outside, it may be. Not in here."

"Then it's just as well I was on my way outside."

"I'll escort you."

If he senses the danger he's in, he doesn't show it. "There's no need."

"Oh, but there's every need." I grip his arm just above the elbow, digging the tip of my thumb into the nerve which runs between the muscle and the bone. To the casual observer it looks like I'm merely steering him in the right direction but the pain is intense, especially for one who prefers dishing it out to taking it. Ethan proves that by letting out a pathetic whine.

"Not so hard!"

"Stop bitching." We're practically flying up the stairs. I'm taking them two at a time and he has no choice but to keep up. Once we reach the ground floor, instead of taking Ethan to the exit, I steer him past the bar and into the back hallway reserved for employee access only.

"Where are you taking me? I thought we were going outside."

"You thought wrong." I punch the code into the keypad and the door to the back stairwell opens. "You think I'm just going to let you go after you violated not one but two guests of this establishment?"

"What do you care? They're only humans." Even now, Ethan is being a haughty prick.

Instead of rising to his bait, I rap on the door to Lucius's office.

"Enter."

Lucius is sitting behind his enormous desk. He takes one look at Ethan and the way I'm gripping him, and raises a single eyebrow.

"Problem?" he says.

"This prick needs to go," I tell him, resisting the urge to shake Ethan. "He assaulted a guest last week and I gave him another chance, told him never to come back. He didn't listen, and went for Leann tonight."

An expression of cold rage comes over Lucius's face. He takes Club Toxic's reputation very seriously. "Do you have anything to say for yourself?" he asks Ethan in a quiet, dangerous voice.

"Fuck you," Ethan spits. "I don't know why you'd get

your panties in a knot over a couple of pathetic little girls. Both of them agreed to play with me."

"Both of them were coerced," I argue, then meet Lucius's gaze. "Do I have your permission to deal with him?"

"Absolutely." Lucius opens a drawer, retrieves a stake, then gets up and walks over to us. Suddenly I'm worried that he's going to do it. I want it so bad I can taste it. This fucker I'm holding assaulted Sabina. *I* want to make him pay.

"Please let me do the honors," I say.

Nothing gets past Lucius. "I get the feeling this is personal," he says.

"Yep." There's no point in lying.

"All right then." He hands me the stake.

"Are you fucking kidding me?" Ethan snarls as soon as he realizes what's about to happen. "You're actually going to *kill* me? For a little thrall?"

I don't bother replying. Instead, I give Lucius a little nod and drag Ethan out of the office and down the stairs. There's a fire exit in the back hallway and I shove it open with my free hand, the stake clenched in my fist.

"Look," my captive begins. His previously dismissive tone now has a note of desperation. I think he's finally realized he's in serious shit he's not going to get out of. "Let's talk about this. I'm sorry, okay? I'll never do it again. I won't come back here."

"You had your second chance. That's more than some get." It's true. Vampires are dangerous. Regardless of what Ethan is promising now, I know he won't stick to it. And even if he never comes back here, he'll only go and hurt women somewhere else. I'm doing the world a favor.

We're outside now, in the private little courtyard which belongs to the club. I drag Ethan between two industrial-sized garbage bins. For the first time, the little fucker really tries to resist me, fighting against my hold on him, trying to wrench his arm free. He's strong.

I'm stronger.

"Any last words?" I ask him.

"Yes. You're pathetic. I can't believe you'd side with some fucking *humans* when our kind should stick together. You should be ashamed of yourself."

I slide the stake into his heart with a swift, smooth thrust, remembering the expression of fear on Sabina's gorgeous face when I first saw her, when she was in this snake's clutches.

I've taken countless lives, but few were ever this satisfying. The light fades from Ethan's eyes and he goes limp. It never fails to amaze me how easy it really is. For all the effort of turning someone, for all the hundreds or thousands of years a vampire can live, his existence can still be snuffed out within seconds. As soon as I let go of Ethan's arm, he slumps to the ground in a suited heap.

"You won't be bothering any guests again now," I say quietly, turning on my heel and leaving his pathetic form right there. Once the sunlight hits his body, he'll disintegrate. Nobody will ever know what happened to him.

As I slip back in through the fire escape and make my way down the stairs into the club proper, my thoughts turn to Sabina. She'll have noticed my absence, no doubt, but that doesn't worry me. She knows I'm working tonight. I never feel remorse or guilt about killing anymore, but for some reason I wonder what she would think if she knew what I'd just done. I can't imagine that she'd condone it. Humans seem to have a different attitude than we do when it comes to death.

Although I suppose that's not surprising, really.

Once I reach the bar, I find Tiberius, who's still

comforting Leann. "I've taken care of it," I tell her. "He won't be bothering you again."

She looks up and I feel a stab of guilt at the expression of misery on her tear-streaked face. "Thank you," she says quietly, but I can almost taste the reproach in her tone. I should have been there. I should have noticed and come to her rescue before it went too far.

"I'm so sorry," I tell her. "Are you going to be all right?"

"Yeah." She gives a little shrug. "Shit happens. I got away before it got too bad."

I'm desperate to go and find Sabina but don't want Leann to feel like I'm abandoning her so soon again after I've let her down.

And this, right here, is why I vowed I'd never get involved with anyone. I can't take care of everyone if I'm focusing all my attention on one person. Sabina is too much of a distraction, and it's preventing me from doing my job properly.

I just don't know whether I can let her go.

I certainly know I don't want to.

20

S*abina*

I'VE NEVER TRIED needles before but after watching that scene unfold, I've decided I'd like to someday. Maybe with Maximus. I make a mental note to ask him but it will have to wait. It's a busy weekend night, and he keeps disappearing from his usual spot on the stool in the corner. Even though I now know this club is full of non-humans, I feel safe here. For one thing, Maximus is never far away, even when he's working. And for another, Zeke won't ever set foot in this building.

Truth be told, he's starting to worry me. I had really thought he would have given up messaging me by now, especially since I never respond. But his showing up at my workplace is freaking me out more, the more I think about it, and while I still don't believe he'd ever actually hurt me,

I'm starting to wonder about what Maximus would do to him if it ever escalated.

Now that I know what happened with Maximus's wife, I can't really say I'm surprised about his protective streak, but even so, that was a long time ago, and I'm a different person. I'm not some insipid nineteenth-century maiden who swoons at the sight of blood. I'm strong, independent, modern. I wish Maximus would realize that. Earlier this week, he convinced me to let him install a GPS tracker on my phone. I still can't believe I let him. My excuse is that I was weak-kneed from our play and feeling tender towards him, and it was just after he told me about Caroline. I figured it wouldn't hurt—I have nothing to hide, after all—and I thought if he did that, he might worry less and loosen his control on me somewhat. I've never met anyone so determined to know about my every movement before. It's kind of sweet, but also a little intimidating, even now that I know where it's coming from.

I catch sight of him at the bar, talking intently to one of his colleagues—Tiberius, I think his name is—and a willowy brunette. Almost as if he can feel me watching him, he turns his head and looks at me. I shoot him a grin but he doesn't return my smile. I wonder if I've done something to upset him, or he's just having a bad night. The brunette certainly doesn't look too happy.

My bag vibrates at my hip and I close my eyes, well aware that there's only one person who would message me at this time of night—aside from Maximus, who's right here with me. Turning around so my back is to the bar and my vampire gladiator (as I've taken to calling him in my head), I fish my phone out of my purse and flick the screen on.

Fucking leech whore.

I stare at the letters, trying to make sense of them. This is the second time Zeke has referred to *leeches* and I wonder what the hell he's talking about. He likes to smoke a joint on occasion, so the first time he used the term, I figured maybe it was a typo or autocorrect of some kind. Twice, however, is too much of a coincidence.

"Zeke?" Maximus's voice in my ear makes me jump about three feet into the air.

"Shit, you scared me!" I stammer.

"Language," he says.

I glare at him, flicking my phone off.

"I asked you a question," he goes on, his voice taking on that low, forceful tone. "Did you get another message from Zeke?"

"Is that girl okay?" I deflect, indicating the direction of the bar with a lift of my chin. "She looked very upset."

"She had a nasty encounter with our old friend, Ethan," Maximus says, and a look of regret flicks over his handsome face.

"Ugh. That slimy creep. He's a vampire too, isn't he?"

"Hush, not so loud." Maximus has explained to me that the majority of club visitors don't know that not all Toxic employees or guests are human. The existence of so many vampires clustered together in Tucson is a closely guarded secret only shared with trusted regulars and lovers. I wanted to ask him why he'd allowed me to find out so soon after meeting him—especially after he told me that they're actually able to wipe a person's mind, essentially removing their memories of a specific event—but if I'm honest, I was afraid of the answer.

"Sorry," I whisper. "Did you find him? Bar him from the club?"

There's a pause. Then, "Let's just say he won't assault any more girls."

A prickle of fear tingles up my spine as his words sink in. "You *killed* him?" Surely he didn't. He wouldn't.

Maximus's face is grim. "I won't lie to you, Sabina. Yes, I did."

The room begins to spin and I wobble. He catches me in a fluid, practiced motion and leads me to the quiet corner where he usually sits. I lean against the wall, trying to process what he's just told me. Even though I've been kind of worried that he'd do the same to Zeke, I don't think I ever really genuinely thought him capable of it until now. I mean, I know he's killed before—he was a soldier, for god's sake—but this is the twenty-first century. You don't just murder a guy because he hassled two women in a nightclub. If everyone did that, there'd be almost no men left in the world.

"Pet?" Maximus has me by the shoulders, watching me intently. "It had to be done. I did warn him not to come back."

"I need a drink." *Or five.* "Could you please get me something strong? A shot?"

"Only if you sit down while you wait for me." He drags over a stool and I perch on it obediently. "Don't move."

I watch him slink off through the throng of club guests, my mind reeling. This past week has been like a dream: insane chemistry, incredible sex, deep tenderness. And I realize that even though I've known what Maximus is for several days now, that knowledge was essentially just theoretical. I romanticized it in my head in order to deal with it. Now, after one simple admission, reality has finally sunk in.

He's a monster. A real life, genuine, bona fide monster.

I look at my surroundings through fresh eyes. The suited, attractive men who are here luring in unsuspecting victims under the guise of BDSM. The stunning women who go with them willingly, usually with no idea of who their play partners really are.

Zeke is a jerk, but he doesn't deserve to die. And if he knows the truth behind this place, even though I can't see how he would have found out, maybe he really is just trying to warn me—to protect me, even though he's going about it entirely the wrong way.

My heart is pounding as Maximus returns holding a glass of amber liquid. Whisky, brandy, I don't care. I take it as soon as he reaches me and drain it in three swallows, relishing the fire as it burns its way down my throat.

"That was very expensive Remy Martin you just guzzled," Maximus says, raising an eyebrow.

"I didn't ask for anything expensive," I retort. "But it was nice, thank you."

He gives me a long, measured look. "You're afraid of me," he says at length. "I can smell it on you."

I'm unable to suppress a snort. "Are you surprised? This kind of thing might be normal for you, but for me, it's..." I trail off, unable to find the right words.

He leans in and once again places his hands on my bare shoulders. His touch sizzles through my flesh, sparking the now-familiar lust deep in my belly, my desire heightened by a whiff of his delicious aftershave and, perversely, the knowledge of just how dangerous he is.

He's no good for me. If I was ever entertaining any notion of an actual relationship with him, I now know that can never happen. *Should* never happen.

"Sabina," he says gently. "I would never, ever hurt you. Everything I do is to protect you—and others. Please don't fear me. I couldn't stand it."

"I don't fear you." Even as I say it I wonder whether

that's true. Mere moments ago, I was thinking about how safe I feel here and with him, whereas now...

"You got another message from Zeke, didn't you?"

Crap. I had hoped he'd forgotten. "Yes, but it doesn't matter."

"Show me."

Maximus can be incredibly stubborn when he wants to be and I know by now that there's no point in trying to dissuade him. "I don't need to show you. I can tell you what it says."

"Go on then." He's frowning down at me and I suddenly feel a wave of resentment. We've only known each other for a week. He knows next to nothing about my life or what I've been through. He's never met Zeke. Yes, I love submitting to Maximus sexually, but we've never had a conversation about starting any kind of relationship, let alone a D/s one. And yet here he is, sticking his oar in everywhere, acting like he owns me. I don't like it.

"Fucking leech whore," I recite, fighting to maintain an even tone. "That's all it said."

Maximus's blue eyes are almost black with fury. A muscle ticks in his jaw.

"Why *leech*?" I say. "And why do I have the feeling you know what he means by that?"

There's a long pause. Maximus just stares at me.

"How come I always have to answer all your questions but you don't always return the favor?" I fold my arms across my chest. "Why *leech*?"

"I'm going to kill him," Maximus says slowly.

"You will do no such thing!" My resentment is slowly building into anger. "Why should you? What has he done to deserve it?"

Maximus looks incredulous. "You're defending him? That dirty sonofabitch?"

"You don't even know him! And no, I'm not defending him; he shouldn't be sending me nasty texts. But that's no reason to kill someone!" My heart is hammering against my ribs now, and I realize I'm as frightened as I am outraged. "God, anyone would think you enjoy killing people!" I pause. "Do you?"

He hesitates for a split second before replying. "Of course I don't."

That tiny pause was enough. "I'm going home," I tell him, sliding off the stool. "I need some time to think."

His huge frame boxes me in, preventing my escape. "Sabina," he growls. "Don't leave. Let's talk this out."

"Please," I say, forcing myself to lower my voice. "I promise we will talk. But not right now. You have to work, and I really need to be alone for a while."

"I don't want you to go," he admits. His tone is softer now, too. "I'm worried about you being alone. After that message—"

"It's not the first message, and it might not be the last. But nothing's happened. Nothing's going to happen. I promise you I can take care of myself. I'm going straight home."

"You've been drinking."

I roll my eyes. "Three sips of brandy." I'm so fired up, it barely had an effect anyway.

"Maximus." A plump woman with a sleek, midnight-black bob has appeared at his shoulder. "Do you have a moment?"

He turns to address her and I seize the opportunity, sliding past him and hurrying towards the stairs. I don't dare look back at him; I can already imagine the way he's glowering.

But I don't care. I'm tired of his constant nagging, his constant implications that I'm helpless, incapable, and unable to look after myself. I've taken care of not only myself but also my siblings for nearly thirty years now, and I don't need some guy I've known for barely a week to appear and tell me I'm incapable of it.

Not to mention the revelations of the past hour. He killed Ethan. Fucking *killed* him! If he did the same to Zeke, I'd never be able to live with myself.

Once in the coat check area, I mumble a quick goodbye to Augustus, who's hovering around there as usual, and make a beeline for the exit. I just want to get home, get into my pajamas, and have some time alone with my thoughts. There's so much to unravel that it's overwhelming me right now.

I also need to figure out how to get Zeke to back off— before it's too late.

21

M aximus

BY THE TIME Laurie has finished bending my ear about Liam and whether he's single, Sabina has vanished.

Fuck.

To say I'm angry would be putting it mildly. I'm incandescent with rage and frustration. How dare she protect that filthy shifter? How dare she judge me for doing her and the rest of the world a favor and getting rid of Ethan? How dare she disobey my direct order not to leave?

I'm on duty but I don't care. Lucius will understand. I thread my way between the people on the dancefloor and find Tiberius at the bar.

"I'm leaving," I tell him. Then, "Where's Leann?"

"I sent her home."

"Is she going to be okay?"

"She'll be fine." Tiberius narrows his eyes. "Can't say the same about you. What's wrong?"

"Nothing. I'm fine."

My old friend lets out a bark of laughter. "Sure you are. I can feel the *fine* tension vibrating off you."

I clench my fists at my sides. "Fuck you."

Tiberius pats the empty stool beside him. "You've been acting weird all week. Why?"

"I have not!" I'm bristling.

"Yes, you have. Even the boss has noticed."

That's hardly surprising. Lucius notices everything.

"What gives?" Tiberius continues. "Are you burned out? Do you need a break?"

The derisive snort escapes me before I can suppress it. "No."

"Does it have anything to do with that delectable blonde I've seen on your arm so often these past few days? What was her name? Sabina?"

The mere mention of her renews my desire to go after her but suddenly the temptation to tell someone about it all, to get a second opinion, is too strong. I sit down heavily on the stool and motion for the girl behind the bar to bring me a beer.

"Yes. Sabina." I sigh.

"She must be special. I've not seen you like this with a woman in a long time."

"I haven't felt like this about a woman in a long time. It scares me," I admit.

"With your history, I'm not surprised," Tiberius says frankly. "So why did she just shoot out of here like a bat out of hell?"

My beer arrives and I take a long swallow. Then I tell him everything: how I met Sabina, about Ethan, Zeke and his messages... right up to the events of this night. "She keeps saying she can handle it," I say at length. "But she has no idea he's a shifter."

"How do you know that?"

"She's not afraid of him. And her reaction when she found out about me—about what we are—I think she would have mentioned it if the second guy she was dating in a row turned out not to be entirely human."

Tiberius contemplates my words for a moment. "I think it was the right thing to let her go. She said she needs some space and time to think. No doubt she feels smothered by you at the moment."

"Smothered?" I bristle again.

"I know you want to protect her but, Maximus, you don't own her. You're not even officially in any kind of relationship with her! She's a grown woman, not a child, and you risk scaring her away if you come on so strong. A GPS tracker? Really?" He scoffs. "Gods. Modern technology."

"I think she's already been scared away," I admit, and the realization that that might be true feels like a rock in my gut. "I killed Ethan for her, and instead of being grateful—"

"She was shocked?" Tiberius finishes for me. "Come on, that surprises you? You need to see things from her perspective. You know humans—normal ones, anyway—don't take that kind of thing lightly. Death is a punishment reserved for the worst of the worst, and even then, there are so many people who don't agree with that. Most countries have abolished the death penalty altogether."

I take another pull of my beer. It's true. England, for one. If what happened to Caroline had happened today, her killers would never have been hanged. They would have been locked up for a few years—fed, clothed, sheltered, given access to a TV. Then they would have been released back into society. The mere idea is nauseating. On the other hand, then I would have been able to avenge her myself...

"I don't doubt that Sabina likes you very much. And it's obvious you care deeply about her," Tiberius says gently. "But it's still early days. She's had her entire world view altered by finding out about our existence. Not to mention, have you ever met this Zeke guy?"

"Haven't had the pleasure yet," I say. "I've seen a picture, though."

"Don't you trust Sabina's judgment at all? If she doesn't believe he'd really harm her, then perhaps she's right."

"Perhaps. Or maybe she's wrong. Caroline obviously thought it was perfectly safe to walk home without waiting for me—" I begin but Tiberius lays a soothing hand on my arm.

"Not to minimize what happened, but that was over a century ago. Different times. Different woman."

I go to take another swig of beer and realize I've already finished the bottle. "This is exactly why I never wanted to fa —get involved again," I mutter, horrified as I realize I was about to say *fall in love*. Was that a slip of the tongue, or is it true? Have I fallen in love with Sabina?

"Why?" Tiberius says. "Love is a wonderful thing. It changes people, usually for the better." He narrows his eyes. "Although I'm not sure that could be said about you specifically. You turn into a possessive, obsessed—"

"Watch it," I growl.

"Be that as it may. If you want my advice, you should give the little blonde some space. By constantly telling her she's unable to look after herself, you're basically insulting her. The same applies to this ex of hers. *She* dated him. She should know him enough to be able to ascertain whether he's an actual threat. By implying she doesn't, you're letting her know you don't trust her."

"I do trust her."

"Fine, you trust her, but you don't trust her judgment."

I chew on that for a moment. As reluctant as I am to admit it, he does have a point. "Maybe you're right. Maybe this is for the best. End it all now, before things go too far."

"End it all?" Tiberius chuckles. "You really are out of practice, aren't you? There is a middle ground, you know—between sticking to someone like glue, and never seeing them again."

"I'm no good for her," I say, realizing with a pang that I truly believe that. "She should meet a nice, human guy who will give her babies and grow old alongside her."

Tiberius rolls his eyes. "She should be the one to make that call, don't you think?"

I suddenly want to be alone with my thoughts. I've been so focused on protecting Sabina from Zeke, not to mention distracted by what she does to me physically, that I've never really thought about what I'd be robbing her of if she stayed with me. I remember having similar discussions with Caroline but that was so long ago and, truth be told, aside from how deeply I loved her, I don't remember much about the rest of our marriage. It was all overshadowed by her brutal death.

"Thanks," I tell him. "For letting me bend your ear."

"Any time."

I get up off the stool and roll my shoulders.

"If you'll let me give you one last piece of advice?" Tiberius asks.

"You'll do it anyway, regardless," I say drily.

"True." He's grinning. "I've known you for a long, long time. I've seen you with countless women but this one is different. And that's special. It's rare to find someone you feel so strongly about—especially when you're as old as we are."

I can feel the corners of my mouth lifting.

"Yes, you've been distracted these past few days but you've also been smiling a lot more. And you say she's a little masochist? That you have great chemistry?"

"Gods, yes," I admit, a pulse of desire shooting through me at the mere thought. "I can't get enough of her in that regard."

"Don't be too quick to throw all that away. Give her a day or two to calm down and process everything. Then talk to her. Be honest about how you feel and find out what she wants."

I finger the phone burning a hole in my pocket, wondering how the hell I'm going to resist contacting her for long enough to give her space. "I can't even message her?"

"I never said that. But if you do, keep it light. Don't ask her where she is or what she's doing. Wish her good night, a good morning, that kind of thing. But hey, that's just my advice. Take it or leave it."

I raise an eyebrow. "Am I really getting advice on how to handle a woman from someone who prefers men?"

Tiberius shrugs. "Love is love."

As I make my way back over to my stool in the corner, his words echo in my mind. *Love.* Do I love Sabina? It's far too soon for that...

Isn't it?

∿

Sabina

. . .

I WAKE up after a restless night feeling like I haven't slept at all. Felix has jumped on my chest and is kneading me intently, purring like thunder. I scratch beneath his chin where he likes it, wincing when he shifts and his claw catches my nipple through the sheet.

"I'm surrounded by sadists," I murmur drily.

Maximus didn't come after me last night. I was sure he would. Not that I wanted him to; I was glad to get a little time to think. Unfortunately, all the thinking I did seems to have led nowhere, as I'm just as confused this morning as I was when I finally dozed off.

Maybe Zeke was right to warn me to stay away from Club Toxic. My life has been nothing but complicated since I went there. And it's only been a damn week.

I need to meet up with Zeke. That's one decision I have made. For one thing, I need to get him to stop messaging me, otherwise Maximus really might hurt him. And for another, he needs to know that that kind of behavior is not okay. Even if I'd never met my vampire gladiator, I'd tell Zeke to back the fuck off.

Reaching out, I pluck my phone from the bedside table. My heart sinks when I see the new message notification, but it's from Maximus. How angry is he that I ran out on him last night? Holding my breath, I open it.

I'm sorry I freaked you out. I've been coming on so strong because I'm worried about you. Sweet dreams, pet.

I blink, stunned, scanning the words twice more to make sure I'm reading them right. I was expecting anger, not remorse. It's a very pleasant surprise.

Felix, apparently irritated that I'm no longer paying any

attention to him, jumps off me and slinks off, presumably to curl up in his favorite box. I often envy him his uncomplicated life. Sleep, eat, groom, poop, repeat. He doesn't have to worry about crazy ex-boyfriends or BDSM clubs full of vampires.

Will I ever get used to that idea? I scramble out of bed and head to the kitchen for some coffee. While it's brewing, I reflect on the way I ran out on Maximus last night. Maybe it was unfair of me. It's no wonder he's so protective after what he's been through. Then again, I'm not his wife. Officially, I'm not even his submissive.

Truth be told, I have no idea what I am to him. A play partner? Something more? What do I *want* to be?

I don't know. Maybe I should get out now, before I'm too attached. It's not like we could realistically have any kind of future together, after all—at least, not one I can picture easily.

You're already attached, a little voice tells me, and I realize I'm holding my phone, my finger hovering over the button to message him. But he'll be asleep now; the sun is high in the sky. I put the phone back down, deciding to text him later.

By the time I've lounged around and drunk some coffee, showered and dressed, put on some makeup and had some toast, I've made up my mind: I need to confront Zeke as soon as possible. Not only do I want it over and done with, but then his messages will hopefully stop and there'll be nothing left to antagonize Maximus, as that's the only thing we really butt heads over at the moment. Also, it's Sunday, and I'm hoping Zeke will be able to carve out some time for me this afternoon.

Taking a deep breath, I get my phone and send him a message asking whether he's free to meet. He replies almost immediately: *So glad you've finally come around. Tonight, 7 pm, the parking lot outside Biscuits.*

I sigh. Seven o'clock is later than I had hoped but at least it's still today. Biscuits is a little diner we had lunch at once. It's not open in the evenings but that's fine, it's not like I want to have dinner with him. I just want to tell him to back the hell off, which shouldn't take more than a couple minutes.

I write back to him: *Okay, see you then.* Then I put my phone down, suddenly aware that my heart is racing. It's just nerves because I haven't seen Zeke since the breakup, I tell myself, but I'm not sure whether that's true. What if Maximus is right and I really am in danger?

"Now you're just being paranoid," I say aloud. Even so, I'm tempted to message Maximus and tell him where I'll be. But that would only guarantee that he'll show up, which is exactly what I don't want. A confrontation between him and Zeke would not end well.

Glancing at the clock, I see that it's almost four in the afternoon. While I'm keen to get this unpleasant meeting over and done with, I also need groceries, so at least I have time to run to the store and back before going to the diner.

Everything will be fine, I reassure myself as I slip on my shoes and make sure I have my wallet, purse, phone and keys. *You're just antsy because Maximus keeps telling you how dangerous Zeke is. But he's one to talk. I doubt Zeke killed anyone yesterday.*

How in the hell did my life get so complicated all of a sudden?

22

S *abina*

MY THROAT IS dry as I watch Zeke get out of his beat-up old Mustang. His dirty-blond hair is shaggy, almost reaching his shoulders, and he's wearing blue jeans and a green and black checkered shirt. I can't help compare him to Maximus, but the difference is like night and day. Looking at Zeke now, I don't know what I ever saw in him.

Smoothing back my hair, which I've got in a casual ponytail, I sling my bag over my chest, then climb out of my own car and walk towards my ex. I deliberately dressed down, not wanting Zeke to think I was trying to impress him. Even so, he rakes me with a long, lingering look as soon as he clocks me.

"Sabina," he says. "You look pretty."

"What do you think you're playing at?" I snap the moment I'm within a few feet of him.

He looks hurt. "What do you mean?"

"Those messages." I put my hands on my hips. "What are you trying to do, scare me? Intimidate me? If you're trying to get me back, you're going about it—"

"Hello to you, too," he interrupts me, the corner of his lip curling up. "Shame you left your manners at home."

"My *manners*?" I clench my fists, forcing my voice to remain calm even though my pulse is racing. "This from the guy who has been threatening me, stalking me—"

"Stalking you?"

"I know it was you outside the clinic the other day."

"I'm looking out for you, baby," he says, and the term of endearment makes me cringe. "You shouldn't have gone to that club. It's dangerous. You have no idea what kinds of people lurk around there." He pauses then, and rubs his chin, dark with dirty blond stubble. "Or maybe you do. I've seen you with that leech. Are you fucking him?"

"Leech? I don't know what you're talking—" I begin, but then everything goes dark and I'm grabbed from both sides. "Zeke, what the fuck?" My voice is muffled and I realize some kind of bag or pillowcase has been shoved over my head. I can't see, and the sudden panic rises like bile in my throat.

"Little leech whores who don't want to learn have to feel," Zeke says, and the icy tone in his voice turns my knees to water. "Put her in my car."

"Wait, Zeke, we can talk about this. You don't have to— put me down!" I shriek as I'm half-carried, half-dragged the short way to his car. I have no idea who's gripping me, who's now opening the rear door and shoving me down until I sprawl across the backseat, but they're strong. It's definitely two guys. Who the hell helps their friend kidnap his ex-girlfriend?

"Shut up, bitch," one of them snarls. "Or we'll gag you."

"She'd enjoy that." Zeke's voice is full of contempt. "You know what those perverts do in that disgusting club."

I can't believe this is happening. Like a worm, I wriggle across the backseat, trying to find the opposite door handle, but as soon as I've reached it, the door opens and someone grabs my wrists.

"Does she like being tied up, too?" I hear, and then rope is looped around my wrists and pulled taut, biting into my skin.

"Wouldn't put it past her."

"Where are you taking me?" I bleat, hating how terrified I sound.

"Somewhere private," Zeke says. The door by my head slams shut again. "Thanks, guys. I can take it from here."

"Are you sure? She seems like a fighter."

"Trust me, I've got it."

I can both hear and feel him getting behind the wheel and I wriggle, struggling to get into a sitting position. "Zeke," I try again. "You don't have to do this. I'm sorry, okay? We can talk about this like adults—"

"Shut up, you little whore!" he barks, startling me into silence. I hear something click and realize that he's locked all the doors.

Shit.

"I don't want to hear another word out of you until we get to where we're going. Someone needs to be taught a lesson."

My mind is reeling, my entire body rigid with panic. I'm almost hyperventilating, the cloth over my face being sucked into my mouth with every breath. *Calm down*, I tell myself, *freaking out is just about the worst thing you can do right now*. He's probably just putting on a show to scare me.

The next moment, death metal music is blaring from all the speakers, pounding through my skull. I've never liked it, and the volume is so high that the car is vibrating with it. Zeke is obviously not in a mood to talk right now.

As he revs the engine and peels away, I force myself to slow my breathing. One thing is for sure: I'm done protecting this asshole. When Maximus hears about this, he's going to want revenge. And I'm going to let him take it.

I have no idea where Zeke is taking me, or how long we've been driving for. It's hard to think straight when your eardrums are bleeding. But at length, the car stops moving and the music is finally cut off. If I wasn't so scared about what was going to come next, I would weep with relief.

The locks click again and the door to my right is opened. I feel the cool air waft over me and wish I could breathe without the fabric clinging to my face. The next moment, my wish is granted as the bag is yanked off my head before I'm tugged out of the car by my upper arm. With my wrists still tied together in front of me, I stand on trembling legs, looking around and trying to get my bearings. We're out in a more rural area; the only building I can see is what looks like a large warehouse.

"Where are we?" I turn to look at Zeke for the first time since the bag was shoved over my head. He's remarkably composed, as if he does this sort of thing all the time.

"Clubhouse," he says curtly, then begins to lead me towards the squat building. There are no lights on inside it, from what I can tell, and the area around us is all dirt and scrub brush. I glance up at the sky and, for a brief second, the beauty of the stars distracts me from this surreal nightmare.

I don't want to enter that warehouse. I have the feeling it won't end well for me. So I stop walking abruptly, buying time, trying frantically to think of a way to escape. "Club-house?" I say casually. "I didn't know you were in a gang."

"There's a lot you don't know about me, Sabina. And it's a shame. I had hoped to be showing you this place under very different circumstances. Still, it is what it is." He begins to propel me forward once more.

"Then tell me," I urge him. "You've got my attention."

He lets out a snort. "*Now* I have your attention. But look what I had to do to get it. Just shut up and get inside." He unlocks the double doors and shoves one of them open.

Dread has settled like concrete in my gut and I enter the building as slowly as I dare, still wondering how the fuck I'm going to get myself out of this mess.

Maybe there's still a way. Maybe Maximus will never have to find out. At this point, I'm not sure what would be worse—his anger with me for putting myself in this situation and not even telling him where I was going, or my humiliation if I end up unable to save myself.

I'm a smart, intelligent adult, I tell myself. Not a damsel in distress. All right, so this isn't quite how I thought my talk with Zeke would go, but so far, nothing too bad has happened. Essentially, I've just been taken to a warehouse out in the wilderness somewhere. Maybe he really is just trying to intimidate me. He's only a guy, and not a very clever one at that. Surely I can outwit him. Play along. Give him whatever it is he wants—or at least let him believe I will.

The cavernous room really does seem to be some kind of clubhouse. There's a rough-hewn bar along one wall boasting a couple of beer taps and there's a shelf behind it holding a few bottles. Worn, filthy, mismatched sofas and armchairs are scattered throughout, and there are two pool tables at the far end. Posters of naked women and a variety of bands paper the walls. It reminds me of a motorcycle club only without the bikes out front.

"So, do you come here often?" I quip, trying to lighten the mood.

"I'm not in the mood for jokes," Zeke snarls, digging his fingertip into my upper arm. "Sit down there and shut up. I'll be doing the talking." He propels me toward a green couch covered in dubious stains and cigarette burns, and shoves me into it. A spring digs into my buttock and my skin feels itchy immediately.

I rest my bound hands in my lap, determined not to show my discomfort, and look up at him as he begins to pace. With his lank hair falling over his eyes and his hands clasped behind his back, he marches back and forth in front of me like a headmaster about to deliver a lecture. A young, grimy headmaster who couldn't command authority over a bunch of kindergarten kids.

"Go on then," I say defiantly. "Talk. If you're not sure where to start, I have a whole bunch of questions." My initial fear has given way to anger. Now his goons have disappeared and it's just the two of us, I feel less worried that he'll actually hurt me, and more livid that he thinks he has any right to treat me this way.

"You know I hate it when you cop an attitude," he growls. "You seemed like such a lady when we met. Now I know you're nothing more than a whore."

Against my better judgment, I answer back. "You keep calling me that, but why? After a few dates with you, I realized we weren't compatible and broke it off. What I've done since then is none of your business but for what it's worth, I've been in touch with one man and he hasn't paid me. So your definition of whore must be different to mine."

"Those leeches are all rich as fuck," Zeke says, spittle

flying off his lips at the expletive. "So maybe they don't pay directly, but no doubt you get nice clothes, expensive dinners, jewelry…"

I let out a bark of mirthless laughter. "Is that so? I must be doing something wrong then. I've had none of those things." I gesture to my blue sweatshirt and gray yoga pants. "Or do I look like a kept woman to you?"

"You didn't dress up for me," he snarls, "but you do for him. I've seen you. High heels, tight dresses, shiny, flowing hair. Wasted on a fucking leech."

"Leech? You keep using that term but I have no idea what you're talking about."

Zeke stops pacing and whirls to face me. His skin is ashen and his eyes are blazing with such loathing, I cringe. "Vampires. Fucking leeches. Bloodsucking undead scum of the earth," he roars. "They should all be staked out in the desert until the sun turns them into dust."

I realize my mouth is hanging open and close it, my thoughts tumbling over one another as I try to digest what he's saying. "So you know," I say slowly. "How?"

"His kind has always hated our kind. And the feeling's entirely mutual." Before I can ask him what the fuck he's talking about—what's Zeke's *kind*?—he continues, "I told you not to go to that club, Sabina. I asked one thing of you. One fucking thing. And you didn't even respect me enough to grant me that."

"I didn't go while we were dating!" I blurt out. "What I did after we broke up is none of your concern!"

"Oh, but it is." He sits down next to me and lays a hand on my thigh. Even though every cell in my body is screaming for me to recoil, I don't want to antagonize him so I force myself to remain still. "I never agreed to break up. It wasn't a mutual decision. Which is why you're still mine. My mate."

"Your mate?" I close my eyes and take a deep breath, wondering when exactly I entered the fucking *Twilight Zone*. "First of all, that's not how breakups work. They don't have to be mutual. If one person decides to end it, that's it. Relationship is over. Secondly, what exactly is *your kind*? I assume you're not a vampire."

I shouldn't have said it but sometimes my mouth runs away with me when I'm mad, and I'm spitting right now. Zeke rewards my snark by squeezing my thigh so hard, I yelp with pain. "Do I fucking look like a fucking vampire to you?" he snarls.

I take in his greasy, limp hair, his unshaven chin, his dirty fingernails, his torn jeans. *Don't do it. Don't say it, Sabina.* "No. You're not nearly groomed or attractive enough."

I hear the slap before I feel it. My ear is ringing, and a hot burn spreads over my left cheek. Still, I refuse to give Zeke the satisfaction of knowing he hurt me. I glare at him, lifting my chin in a show of defiance.

"One more comment like that, slut, and I'll call my friends over here to take turns on you," Zeke says in a low, furious voice. "Maybe I'll get that leech of yours over here to watch."

I've seen how fast Maximus can move. I know he can—and will—kill without hesitation. "Do it," I challenge Zeke. "Call him over here. I guarantee you that not one of your slimy, shitty friends would survive the night."

"Don't be so sure," Zeke retorts. "Leeches aren't the only ones with special abilities."

Once again, I wonder what the hell he's talking about. "So what are yours? Aside from being an asshole?"

Grabbing my chin, he turns my face so I'm looking directly at him. It takes a moment for me to see it but when I do, a cold fear prickles over my skin. His pupils, instead of being round, are suddenly vertical slits in his green irises. Like a cat's. *What the fuck?* "Nice contacts," I say, trying to hide how freaked out I am, but then he blinks and his pupils grow round again. "What are you?"

"I'm a shifter. I can turn into a cheetah."

At first, I'm not sure I heard him correctly. "A cheetah? Like the big cat?"

"Yes, like the big cat." He rolls his eyes. "Many of us have settled here. Our packs include bears, wolves, even rarer animals like owls, gorillas—"

It's all too much. The bubble of laughter rises up in my chest and bursts out of me before I can stop it. I cackle maniacally, and the look of angry disbelief on Zeke's face only serves to make me laugh harder. It takes me several moments to get a grip on myself. "You're seriously expecting me to believe that, as well as a nest of vampires, Tucson hosts several packs of *shifters?* What, is this the secret supernatural capital of the world? Do the tooth fairy and Santa live in Arizona as well?"

At that, Zeke lets out a primal, animal snarl which sounds just like the big cat he's purporting to be. It's fierce and inhuman, and my mirth dies instantly.

"You're not kidding," I whisper, fear once again gripping my gut. "It's really true?"

"It's nice to see you finally giving me the respect I deserve," Zeke says coldly.

I realize my thighs are trembling and jam them together to hide how unnerved I am. "I have so many questions," I say, trying to distract him.

"I'm not here to answer your questions," he snaps. "You're here to answer mine."

"All right," I say, defeated. If he can really shift into a fucking cheetah, he's a lot more dangerous than I thought. Does Maximus know about this? Was this why he was so worried?

I want to kick myself for being so stubborn. For not telling him I was meeting Zeke. For not listening to his warnings. And I know what I have to do.

Looking up at Zeke as seductively as I can, I say, "I'll answer your questions. But would it be okay if I go to the bathroom first? Nature calls. I assume you have a bathroom in here..."

He indicates a door towards the back of the building. "Just the one. It's the men's, so don't expect any flowers or shit." I wonder what he thinks ladies' rooms are like. Classical music, lace doilies and bouquets of fresh roses? "I won't," I say drily. "I'll be quick." I hold out my bound wrists. "Could you untie me first?"

"No chance," he says, getting off the sofa and hauling me to my feet. "You'll manage somehow. And I'll be right outside, so don't even think about pulling any tricks. We're a long way from town, and I have the car keys right here." He pats his jeans pocket. "You won't get far if you try to run. I'll have caught you and called my friends before you even make it off the property."

"Jeeze, I just need to use the bathroom," I mutter. "I'm not planning any kind of escape."

"Just wanted to warn you." We've reached the back of the room now and he shoves the door open for me. "And hurry it up."

"I'd be quicker if you untied me, but I'll go as fast as I can."

"And no locking the door. I can kick it in anyway."

"All right, there's no escape! You've made your point! God. Can I go pee now?" Without waiting for a reply, I push the door shut in his face, yank my pants and panties down and squat over the bowl. No doubt he'll be listening. Then I fish my phone out of my purse. My hands are shaking so much, it takes me a couple of tries before I've selected Maximus from my list of contacts. I hit *new message*, then type out my cry for help before pressing send.

I can only pray he'll see it in time, and that the software he installed works the way he said it would.

Otherwise, I'm fucked.

23

M *aximus*

ANGER DOESN'T EVEN BEGIN to come close to describing the emotion I'm experiencing right now. I am livid. Furious. Incandescent with rage, both at that little cocksucker Zeke, and at Sabina, for not listening to me.

It was right after sunset and I was just waking up, groggily making a coffee, when I received her text message. For a second I stared at it, wondering whether I was reading it right. Then I leapt into action.

Now I'm gripping the steering wheel of my car, speeding down the highway like a bat out of hell, little white spots dancing across my vision.

I'm going to kill Zeke.

And then...

What then?

After Caroline, I vowed never to feel this way again.

Then that little blonde opened a tiny fissure in my heart and I let her—only for her to blatantly disobey me and put herself in harm's way. If she's still okay—and I won't know until I reach the location her GPS tracker is indicating on my app—I don't know whether I'll ever be able to trust her again. Is love really worth going through this kind of fear?

I wish I could make my car blur but all I can do is press the gas pedal to the floor as I eat up the miles. The red circle on my app indicating Sabina's location is getting larger.

Thank fuck I installed this software on her phone. If I hadn't...

Well, that doesn't even bear thinking about.

The text message she sent me is imprinted into my brain. *I went to meet Zeke, now he's holding me at some club-house. Please find and rescue me. I'm sorry.*

What has the fucker done to her? Does she know he's a shifter yet? Why would she willingly go and meet with him?

Gods, and all this before I've even had one sip of coffee.

I'm so rigid with fury that I almost miss the tiny dirt road on my right, and have to back up before turning onto it. Another half mile or so and I can see the squat building. It's in the middle of nowhere, out in the tundra—exactly the kind of place shifters like to hang out.

There's only one car parked out front: a shitty Mustang. Presumably Zeke's. It's all I can do not to smash the fucking windshield as I hustle past it once I've parked my own vehicle and jumped out.

Is he alone in there with her, or are there more? Shifters generally like to roam in packs. But Sabina wrote he's *holding me*, not *they*.

I'm about to find out.

It might be prudent to scope the place out first, peep through the windows, try to find out what scenario awaits me inside. But I can't. I'm too mad and hyped up. It's very rare that I lose control, and I don't like the feeling, but right now my aggression might serve me well.

The ramshackle door flies open easily after I give it a swift kick. There's a resounding bang as it hits the wall, and I'm through it before it can rebound.

I take in the entire scene within the time it takes for Sabina and Zeke to look up.

The dirty fucker is sprawled on top of her on a filthy sofa, and when his eyes meet mine, I see the slitted, vertical pupils. Sabina's hands are bound in front of her, and her beautiful face is a mask of terror.

"Maximus!" she cries. The way she says my name is half a sob and the sound goes right through me, spurring me into action.

Before Zeke knows what's hit him, I'm on him, yanking him off the couch and flinging him halfway across the room. I could just snap his neck but I want the fucker to suffer first.

He lets out a snarl and I realize he's about to shift.

"Run outside, Sabina," I tell her, not wanting her to see what I'm about to do. But she remains frozen in place. "Fucking NOW!" I roar, and she finally moves. I can't stop and wait to see whether she actually goes all the way outside. "I'm going to kill you," I tell Zeke, who has bounced up off the floor and is baring his teeth at me. His incisors have already grown into sharp points. I don't care. I have fangs of my own.

"You can fucking try, you little leech," he growls.

"I'm gonna do more than that." The stench of both his stale and fresh sweat is overpowering as I launch myself at and land on him, knocking him back down to the ground. His skull bashes the floor, hard, and I begin to punch his face over and over, venting all the anger that's boiling inside me, relishing the crunch of cartilage and bone giving way.

The blood coating my knuckles is sticky and warm.

"Maximus, stop!" Sabina cries, and I turn to glare at her.

"I told you to—"

Zeke seizes his chance and sinks his teeth into my arm.

Roaring with pain and rage, I drive my knee into his belly, forcing him to release me before I grab his head with both hands and twist with all my might.

The crack is audible as his neck snaps and he goes limp.

"Fucker!" I spit, staring down at him, still straddling him, disappointed I didn't make him suffer more.

A soft whimper reaches my ears and I turn to see Sabina. She's cowering against the wall, and her skin is the color of fresh milk. She's trembling. "You killed him," she whispers.

"You weren't supposed to see that." I get to my feet slowly and the burning pain in my arm makes me look down to see the blood dripping to the floor. He didn't just bite me; he tore a chunk of flesh off me between my wrist and elbow.

"You're hurt," she adds, rather unnecessarily.

"It's nothing." If this were a movie, she'd be in my arms now, flushed and swooning, kissing me passionately, grateful beyond measure that I saved her from the bad guy.

This isn't a movie. She's still staring at me warily from across the room, and the fear in her eyes is hurting me more than any physical pain ever could.

"It probably needs stitches," she says.

I let out a dry chuckle. "Sure. Let's head on over to the nearest ER and tell them I got bitten by a cheetah, shall we? Don't worry about it, pet. It's not like it will kill me."

My attempt to lighten the mood falls pitifully short. The

blood is dripping steadily onto the ground, and I'm starting to feel a bit woozy. Just because I can't die doesn't mean I don't feel pain. Or I can't pass out from lack of blood. Fuck.

"Sabina," I say softly, injecting just a hint of my dom tone into my voice. "I know you're in shock right now but I need your help. Please. You don't need to be afraid. Everything will be okay."

"I just..." She trails off.

"We can talk about all this later. Right now, we need to act. I need you to help me stop this bleeding. Please."

"How?" She takes a tentative step towards me, then another.

Atta girl.

"Come here. Please, pet." *I saved you*, I want to add, but something tells me she won't be seeing it that way—at least, not yet.

After what feels like an eternity, she reaches my side. I can smell the fear emanating from her entire body and the thought that I'm causing it is almost my undoing. She's deliberately avoiding looking down, where Zeke's limp form is still sprawled on the floor, his head cocked at an unnatural, gross angle.

"Give me your hands," I coax her. They're still bound together but I slice the rope with my fangs and help unwind it from her wrists. Her fingers are almost blue and she rubs them immediately. "Are you okay?"

"No!" She lets out a noise which sounds like a half-hiccup, half-sob.

"You're right, it was a stupid question," I admit. "But you're strong and brave, and I need you to stay that way, at least for a little longer."

"What do you need me to do?"

"I'm bleeding out here, pet. I know it's a lot to ask but if you would let me feed from you, that would really speed up my healing process."

Her expressive blue eyes are huge and round as she gazes at me. "And if I don't?"

"I'll probably pass out." There's no point in lying to her.

"Oh god!" The worry in her tone is comforting. She still cares. Thank the gods. She takes my uninjured hand and steers me to the sofa. "Come and sit down."

I'm growing impatient. There's no telling when some random shifter—or group of them—will turn up here at the clubhouse and find their shitty, dead little friend. I need to feed, then I have to hide the body. Then we need to get the fuck out of here. But I can't rush Sabina. She's too freaked out as it is. So I sink down on the couch and wait while she takes a seat beside me. I could feed from Zeke but the mere idea of it makes me want to puke.

The edges of my vision are starting to get blurry and the familiar fatigue which sets in when I've over-exerted myself is beginning to settle into my very bones. "Sabina," I say again. "Will you help me?"

"I'm scared," she admits. "We've never done it without..."

She doesn't need to finish the sentence. Every time I've sipped from her in the past, it was while she was climaxing.

"Would it help if you were feeling pleasure at the same time?" I offer, wondering where I'm going to find the strength.

"No, I don't think I could right now. But... will it hurt?"

I almost smile. "You telling me you're afraid of pain?"

She lets out a soft chuckle. "I guess that was a dumb question."

"Please help me, pet."

"I was so scared for you!" she blurts out suddenly.

The raw emotion in her tone gives me courage and I

lean over and press my lips to hers, suddenly desperate to show her what she means to me. "I was terrified when I got your message," I admit. "If I'd been too late... did he hurt you badly?"

"Not as badly as he hurt you." She lets out a little sigh. "God, I'm so relieved. I thought you'd be furious!"

I don't want to lie to her but I don't want to get into a discussion right now, either. "Sweetheart, I don't mean to rush you but we're in a bit of a precarious position at the moment. We can talk about everything later." I look down at the blood dripping from my arm and her eyes follow my gaze, widening when they see the extent of my injury.

"Oh god, sorry, of course! Here!" Her hair is up in a ponytail so her neck is already bared when she leans in. "I'm sorry I wasted so much time!"

"It's okay, baby, you're in shock." I caress her nape with my uninjured hand, then grip her ponytail and yank her head back. Her gasp is one of arousal, just as I intended, and despite everything, it goes straight to my groin.

The sweet taste of her blood coating my tongue is a high unlike any other and I drink eagerly, feeling my strength and energy return with every beat of her pulse. Her hair is like silk against my palm and she's moaning softly, shuddering, probably feeling the effects of the serum I'm slipping into her.

Once I've drunk enough to be able to function, I lap at the puncture marks on her pale skin before coating a fingertip in my own blood and dabbing it on her wounds.

"Are you okay, pet?" I murmur, stroking her cheek.

Her eyes are half-lidded and she looks dazed. "Mmmn."

"Thank you for that," I tell her. "I feel much better. And look, it's already stopped bleeding. You just rest here for a moment, okay? And then we'll go home."

"Yes, Sir."

Now that my injury is no longer at the forefront of my mind, the previous jumble of emotions has returned. *Yes, Sir.* Those two little words went straight through me, making a warm sensation pool in my gut, but I'm also still battling anger with her for getting herself into this situation, and fear—for her safety, for the future, for my own sanity.

First things first: clear up my mess. One thing at a time. Leaving Sabina curled up on the couch, I get to work, forcing thoughts about anything else to the back of my mind.

The longer I can put off what will no doubt be an incredibly difficult discussion, not to mention an even harder decision, the better.

24

S *abina*

I FEEL like I'm in some kind of waking nightmare but the details are all so vague, and everything seems almost too surreal.

Maximus killed Zeke. Zeke kidnapped me. Zeke was a shifter. A cheetah. I'm curled up in the passenger seat of Maximus's car, watching the occasional light flash past the black window, trying in vain to wrap my head around the events of this evening. Glancing to my left, I study Maximus's handsome profile. He's staring straight ahead, and there's a muscle ticking in his jaw. I had thought he would be more angry with me for going to see Zeke behind his back but there's been no sign of that at all. Is it still coming?

"You okay?" I ask softly.

"I've had better evenings."

His arm is wrapped in a strip of material torn from his t-shirt, and my fingers go to the puncture wounds on the side of my neck. Who knew human blood could help vampires heal faster?

Who knew I would ever be sitting in a car with a vampire, even *thinking* that?

"I'm sorry," I begin, wanting to get this conversation over with before we get to the diner where my car is still parked and I potentially lose my chance to apologize. "I just wanted to ask him to back off. I was meeting him in a public place. I had no idea—"

"That he was a shifter?"

The edge in Maximus's voice makes me want to shrink back into the seat. Shit, he really is angry. Once he'd taken some of my blood and recovered himself somewhat, I'd basically passed out on the sofa while he took care of Zeke's body. I don't know what he did with it. I don't want to know. Buried it somewhere outside, I assume, judging by the way he looked when he came back into the clubhouse. "That he was a shifter," I confirm.

I put him into this position. This is all my fault. It's all too much to even wrap my brain around. I want to wind the clock back to this afternoon. No, scratch that. I want to wind it back a couple weeks, to where I never met Ethan, never met Maximus, never found out about vampires, shifters...

"We'll discuss it when we get home," Maximus says curtly.

"Home? My car is parked—"

"We're not stopping for your car right now. We're going to my place, which is closer, and then we're going to have a little talk. We can pick up your car afterwards."

If I'm even still alive to drive it, I think glumly, once again turning to stare out of the window. There's a knot of anxiety in the pit of my stomach, and I keep having these shaking fits. Leftover adrenaline, probably, not unlike the ones I get after an intense scene.

Of course all this had to happen after I'd already had a fight with Maximus. It's just poured fuel onto the fire. I was mad at him because he was behaving like he owns me when we haven't even yet labeled this thing between us, and he was mad at me because I didn't want him to get involved in my situation with Zeke.

God, I should have listened to him. And that's almost the worst part of all.

By the time we roll up Maximus's long driveway and into his huge garage, you could cut the tension between us with a knife. Wordlessly, he gets out, and comes around to my side but I've already opened the door and am standing beside it. We head into the kitchen and I realize my heart is pounding; the knot of anxiety has turned into a rock in my belly.

"I need to take a quick shower," he says, indicating the reddish brown dirt streaking his clothes, arms, and face. "Get yourself a drink if you want, and then we'll talk."

His voice is so cold, so different to how it was before. To how it is usually when he speaks to me. It's frightening. I take a step towards him. "Maximus," I say gently, wanting to lay a hand on his arm but not daring to. "I really am sorry."

He must be able to hear the fear in my tone because his face softens slightly, giving me a spark of hope. "I know," he says. "We'll talk in five."

As soon as he's disappeared upstairs, I make my way to the bar in the lounge room, fishing out a bottle of vodka. Being in there reminds me of the first time I was here. The effect Maximus had on me. The butterflies I had in my stomach. Before I knew what he really was.

Pushing that thought down, I head into the kitchen to find a glass and some tonic.

Where do we go from here? I wonder as I down my drink in just a few swallows and pour myself a second. I try to let the different scenarios play out in my head, examining my feelings as I do so. The one where we fight and decide never to see each other again is by far the most painful and terrifying. Something changed tonight, and even though the knowledge is there, deep down inside me, I'm not prepared to examine it fully, let alone admit it.

Frankly, I'm way too scared.

It's not long before Maximus's voice interrupts my thoughts.

"All right, I'm back. Can you pass me a beer, please?"

I reach into the fridge for a Bud Light and hand it to him. His hair is wet and there are still droplets of water on his broad, beautiful shoulders. He's wearing a black sleeveless tee and gray sweats. His feet are bare. It's all I can do not to run into his arms. He eyes my glass. "Still your first?"

I shake my head. "Second."

"Better make it last. Come on then." Without waiting, he walks off into the den.

I follow, my heart in my mouth, my mind racing. *Let him take the lead,* I tell myself. *You fucked up, you disobeyed him. You saw how scared he was. You did that to him.*

That was the worst part of the entire evening: the fear on his face when he walked into the clubhouse and saw me there with Zeke on top of me. It must have brought the whole Caroline scenario right back to him.

Why was I so fucking stupid?

He folds himself into the couch and points to a nearby armchair. "Sit," he orders.

I sink into the plush seat.

"Where to begin?" he continues after a brief silence. "First of all, are you okay? You've had a nasty shock. If you want to table this discussion for another time, let me know. While I was in the shower, I realized you might not be in the right frame of mind—"

"No," I interrupt him. "I appreciate the sentiment but I want to get this over with."

His eyebrow lifts, and he takes a pull of his beer. "Very well then. Do you want to tell me exactly what happened?"

No, I'd rather crawl over a mile of broken glass. Taking a deep breath, I recount everything as briefly as possible—how I wanted to get Zeke to back off, arranged to meet him at the Biscuits parking lot, how his friends helped him kidnap me, and what happened once we arrived at the clubhouse.

Maximus's face is growing darker and darker. Even though he's a few feet away, I can feel the fury emanating off him. "And what happened in the time after you messaged me but before I arrived?"

"Just more of the same. He was insulting me, telling me what he wanted to do to me, accusing me of being a whore, of associating with you and Club Toxic..." I trail off, not wanting to remember.

"He touch you?"

"He shook me a couple times, slapped my leg." *Squeezed my breast,* but I won't tell Maximus that. "But nothing too bad."

Maximus lets out a little huff. "Nothing too bad," he repeats under his breath.

"I'm so sorry!" I blurt out, desperate to somehow let him know how much I regret everything. "I should have listened to you. You were right, I was wrong. I thought I could handle it, thought I could handle him, and put myself in danger. You must have been worried, and I—"

"Worried?" he snarls, interrupting me. Leaping off the couch, he begins to pace. "Sabina, you are the most beautiful, fascinating, sensual, intelligent, infuriating woman I've ever met. From the first moment I saw you, I wanted you. To spend time with you, to get to know you, to protect you. You do things to me I can't even..." He trails off and shoves a hand through his cropped black hair. "I tried to fight it because of what I am, because of how I am. And because I was afraid. It's been a fucking *century* since I let myself love anyone because I knew I would not be able to handle going through that kind of grief and loss again. And then, when you sent me that text, when I got into the clubhouse and saw that fucker sprawled on top of you, I realized..."

He stops and I realize I'm leaning forward, clutching my still full glass, tears blurring my vision. "You realized what?" I whisper, my voice breaking.

"That it was too late," he says, resignation in his tone. His shoulders are slumped in defeat. "I love you."

I can hardly believe what I'm hearing. I get to my feet, realizing how watery my knees are as soon as they take my weight. Setting the glass down carefully on the coffee table, I approach him slowly. Once I'm within reaching distance, he turns and looks at me. His gorgeous eyes are sad, and guilt crushes me for causing him this kind of turmoil.

"I love you too," I whisper. "I promise, if you give me another chance, I'll never put you through that kind of worry again. I'll always obey you when you warn me about situations. I know it's crazy, because we've only known each other such a short time, but I can no longer imagine my life without you in it."

Maximus reaches out, grips the nape of my neck, and

yanks me to him, crushing his lips to mine in a breathtaking, torrid kiss. Instantly, every nerve ending in my body lights up but even as I try to relax into it, I realize I can't.

After a few moments, he pulls away. "What's wrong?"

I shake my head, blinking back the tears. "I feel so guilty," I whisper. "I should have listened to you, Sir. I don't feel like I deserve pleasure right now."

A little frown appears in the center of his forehead as he considers my words. "Do you feel like you deserve to be punished?"

As he says it, I realize how much I do. How badly I want to atone for putting him through what I did. "Yes. But this isn't about me. Do you want to punish me?"

"I'm not gonna lie, pet, even though I've calmed down, I'm furious with you. If I do punish you, it will not be the least bit pleasurable. But afterwards, I'd like to wipe the slate clean and start again. No more secrets. No more with-holding things." He caresses my cheek and I realize I'm trembling. "I want to know everything about you. Why you feel such a need to be strong and independent. Why you fight against the idea of letting a man—me—protect you. And yes, as long as you're mine, I need you to obey me in all rules I set to keep you safe. No exceptions. Understood?"

"Yes, Sir."

"Good girl." He leans down to kiss me again and this time I kiss him back with abandon, relishing the feel of his tongue against mine, the way he runs his fingers through my hair and tilts my face back so he can take it deeper. He tastes faintly of beer, and his delicious aftershave, as always, makes me weak at the knees.

After a long, long time, by which point I'm so aroused I'm barely able to stand upright, he pulls away. His expression is serious, his eyes searching. "I'm going to take you home now," he says.

"Wait, what?" I'm stunned.

"It's late, and you have work in the morning. We'll go pick up your car, and then I want you to go directly home, have something to eat if you can, and go straight to bed."

"I thought—"

"Don't interrupt me, pet."

I drop my gaze. His tone of voice is sterner than I've ever heard it.

"I want you to think long and hard about whether you want to be with me. Whether you're willing to accept what that entails. I'm a vampire. I cannot father children. We will never be able to relax on a sunny beach together, have daytime picnics, go to an amusement park. While I don't enjoy killing, I won't hesitate to do so if I feel it's necessary and sometimes, unfortunately, it is. I'm protective to the point where it might feel overbearing."

He's not wrong there, I think wryly, but I remain silent, listening.

"Due to the nature of my job, I spend a lot of time with women. Sometimes they're naked. If a girl is in danger in the club, I will intervene and help her, and she may not always be clothed. I can't stop and worry about whether you'd feel jealous."

"It feels like you're trying to warn me off you," I mutter, no longer able to keep quiet. "If you don't want me, just say so."

"For fuck's sake!" With a growl, he yanks me to him, crushing my entire body against the length of his. "You feel that?" He grinds his pelvis against me and there's no mistaking how rigid his big cock is. "I want you. I fucking *love* you, Sabina. But I won't do half-measures with you anymore. If we go ahead with this, I want you to know exactly what to expect."

"All right," I whisper. "Please go on."

"You may feel jealous at times, but I promise you, there's no need. You're the most beautiful, fascinating, infuriatingly wonderful girl I've met in a long, long time, and I want to love you, protect you, cherish you and make you happy in every way I can." He thrusts slowly, his hard length grinding against my sex through our clothing, and I gasp as a flood of desire rushes between my legs. "But in order for it to work, you have to do three things: trust me, obey me, and accept me for who I am."

"Yes, Sir," I whisper.

"Good girl." He takes a step back and I already feel the loss. I want him back in my arms. "So here's what's going to happen. You're going to go home and think very carefully about whether you want this. Whether you want *me*. If you do, I will pick you up tomorrow night at eight pm and take you to Toxic, where you will be publicly punished, and then collared."

"What?" My mind is spinning, my heart threatening to pound its way right out of my ribcage.

"That way, everyone will know you belong to me," he says. "The punishment won't be pleasant, like I said, but it won't be anything you can't take. You want to atone, and I want to make you. And then I can make you mine in front of everyone. If, on the other hand, you decide you'd rather not continue our relationship, you have until seven tomorrow evening to let me know. It will break my heart but I'll understand. The ball is in your court, pet."

I already know I want to be with him; I can't imagine telling him no. But to be punished in front of everyone? "Does the punishment have to be public, Sir? I'm afraid."

He strokes my cheek with a gentle finger. "Do you trust me, Sabina?"

"Yes."

"Good. Agreeing to this will be the first way you can prove that to me."

All I want is for him to take me in his arms and then take me to bed, but instead he presses one last brief kiss against my lips, and heads into the kitchen for his car keys.

When Maximus makes his mind up about something, there's no changing it.

All I know is that I'm in for a sleepless night, and that tomorrow will feel like the longest day of my life as I wait for the sun to set.

25

M aximus

THE MOMENT I opened my eyes after waking up, I reached for my phone. After giving Sabina the ultimatum and dropping her off at her car, I spent the rest of the night worrying and pacing. Was it too much pressure? Would the threat of public punishment be what unraveled any chance of a future together? Maybe I should have thought everything through more carefully but then again, I wasn't lying when I said I loved her, and I dislike half measures. Either she'll be mine, or she won't. No more obeying my rules during a scene and then going off and doing whatever she likes— putting herself in danger—whenever I'm not beside her.

To my immense relief, there was no message on my phone, so she hadn't texted to cancel. I had given her specific instructions to only send me a text if she decided she didn't want to go ahead with the relationship. If I didn't hear from her by seven, I would assume she was expecting me to pick her up at eight.

Which is why I'm now walking up the neat little pathway leading to her condo, wearing my best charcoal-grey suit, holding a huge bunch of long-stemmed red roses. My heart is in my mouth, and I feel absurdly like an inexperienced youth going on his first date, which is ridiculous for a man of my age for a whole number of reasons. Still, I can't stop the grin from tugging at the corners of my mouth, and have to force my expression to be stern when she opens the door.

If I were still human, the sight of her would take my breath away. Her long, gorgeous blonde hair is trailing over bare shoulders. A tight black halter neck top stops just beneath her pert, high breasts, displaying her smooth midriff. A purple and black lacy miniskirt shows off her long legs, which seem even longer due to the mauve high heels she's wearing.

"You look stunning, pet," I say, and lean in to drop a brief kiss on her glossy pink mouth.

"Thank you, Sir." The fear in her voice makes me ache to pull her into my arms but instead I hand her the roses. "Oh wow, they're gorgeous! Ow! Thorn!" She sucks at her finger and my cock twitches at the sight. "I'll just go and put them in a vase."

"Actually, I want you to bring them to Toxic with you," I tell her. Then, when she looks confused, "We'll need them for the ceremony."

"All right. Bye, Felix." She crouches down and gives her cat a quick rub between the ears before picking up her bag and slinging it over her shoulder. "I assume you're driving?"

"You assume correctly."

She closes the door behind her and we make our way to

my Rolls. "Wow. Roses and a Rolls Royce. Pulling out all the stops tonight, I see!"

"Only the best for you, my love."

I open the passenger door for her and, after putting the roses in the back, she slides into the seat, her smooth, bare thighs creamy against the dark leather. I can still hardly believe my luck—by the end of this evening, this stunning creature will belong to me.

"How was your day?" I ask as we pull out into the traffic.

"Long. Nerve-wracking," she admits. "I couldn't stop worrying about the punishment."

I knew that would be the case. In fact, the anticipation was part of the punishment, but she doesn't need to know that. "You trust me, don't you?"

"Yes, Sir."

"I'm not saying it will be pleasant, but you asked to atone. Or has your guilt disappeared?"

"Oh no, not at all!" There's genuine sincerity in her voice. "I don't think I'll feel better about... what happened... until I really feel like I've made it up to you, but I'm still nervous. I think it's more the case of it being public."

Again, I knew that, which was why I decided her punishment should take place in one of the open play areas rather than in a booth. "You like watching public scenes," I say, remembering the ecstatic expression on her face when she observed the needle session the other night. "Just think of it this way: you'll be giving others that same kind of pleasure tonight."

"I guess so." She leans back in her seat and sighs. Reaching out, I place a hand on her thigh. Her flesh is warm and I have to fight the urge to slide my fingers up between her legs.

"You'll be wonderful, pet. I'll be the proudest man there. Now, were you a good girl last night? Did you obey me?"

"Yes, Sir. It was hard, but I did."

"I'm pleased to hear it. And you remember why you were given that instruction?"

Yesterday evening, after taking her to her car in the deserted diner parking lot, I edged Sabina for ten full minutes. Any innocent passersby would have simply seen a couple kissing passionately, but in fact my fingers were inside her pants on her taut, throbbing little clit, rubbing, pinching and caressing it until she was on the brink of climax, then easing off—again and again, until her panties were drenched and she was begging me incoherently, her pleas muffled by my lips and tongue. Then I sent her home with firm instructions not to masturbate or come until *I* gave her her next orgasm. Another part of the punishment. I do so enjoy torturing girls in that way.

"Because I'm being punished, and bad girls don't deserve to orgasm," she whispers, and my cock jerks in my suit pants. I have a lot planned for this evening, and I don't want to be distracted by my own arousal, so I wait for the next suitable spot and pull into it, parking the car in a deserted layby.

"What are we doing, Sir?"

"You're going to please me," I tell her, unzipping my pants. I need to be able to focus on the scene tonight, and this will help take the edge off so I can concentrate. "Pull your skirt up around your waist and kneel on the seat, facing me."

Sabina complies, and a few moments later her lips are wrapped around my length. She's on her hands and knees, her bare ass up in the air, pointed at the window. I had instructed her not to wear any panties so now I can see her cunt in the reflection. I grip her hair in my fist, guiding her movements for a while before I grow impatient and hold her head in place while I fuck her throat.

The sight of her so exposed to anyone who might happen to wander by, as well as the delicious sounds she's making as she gags on my cock, combine to make me come in record time, and I keep her face steady as I pump my seed into her mouth, telling her to be a good little slut and swallow it all.

Once I've finally finished throbbing, I release her and tell her she may pull her skirt back down. Her face is flushed, and her eyes have that glazed look they get when she's aroused. Gods, but I love this woman and her sexual obedience.

"You did well," I tell her, tucking my cock back into my pants as she settles back into her seat. "Did you enjoy that?"

"I did, Sir."

"Good girl. Now buckle up."

Once she's put her seatbelt back on, I start up the engine. We're only a few minutes away from the club. Now that the pounding ache in my groin has subsided, I can concentrate on the task ahead of me.

This beautiful girl beside me needs to be punished for what she put me through, and I intend to make sure she will think twice about putting herself at risk in future.

But she'll be brave, and strong, and she'll take it, and then I will proudly put my collar on her, showing everyone at Toxic that she's mine.

I can't wait.

～

Sabina

. . .

JUST AS I HAD PREDICTED, today felt like the longest day of my life. Not because my decision was hard, though. Even as Maximus gave me the ultimatum yesterday, I knew what my answer would be. There was no longer any doubt in my mind that I wanted to be with him. To give it a go, see whether we had any chance together. And I agree with him about no longer wanting half measures. I prefer our relationship to be clearly defined.

You can't get much more clearly defined than a collar.

But first I need to get through the punishment, and the thought of that is what made it nearly impossible for me to focus on work today. I don't even really think it matters what Maximus does to me—the fact that it will be public, and the reason why I'm being punished are what are weighing so heavily on my soul.

I was beyond relieved when he suggested giving me a chance to alleviate at least some of the guilt I feel for going to see Zeke behind his back. The look of fear on Maximus's face when he burst into the clubhouse shook me to my core. After what he went through with Caroline, it must have been like reliving your worst nightmare, and I'm willing to do anything to make up for it.

Which is why I'm gripping his hand now as I follow him into Club Toxic on watery knees and the heels I swore never to wear again. It's a Monday night, so I didn't expect it to be very busy, but there are still way too many guests for my liking when we arrive down in the dungeon level.

He has a confident stride, briefly greeting those he knows as we pass them but not stopping to make small talk. His toybag is slung over his shoulder and I try not to look at it. God only knows what he has in store for me.

Once we've reached the bar, he orders a double gin and tonic and tells me to lay the roses on the stool beside me. I obey, grateful beyond measure that he's allowing me this one drink to take the edge off. He already knows me so well.

"I'm just going to sort out the scene area," he murmurs in my ear, his lips brushing my skin and making me shiver. "Wait here for me and enjoy the drink, it will be your last for a while."

"Yes, Sir."

Such is his commanding presence that people's heads turn to look at him as he makes his way across the dance floor, and I feel my heart swelling with pride. He's my man, I think incredulously. Undoubtedly, many women desire him, and yet he's here with me. It's almost enough to distract me from what's about to happen.

Almost.

I force myself to sip my drink even though I'm tempted to guzzle it. Despite my nerves, I'm also incredibly turned on, not just because of the orgasm restriction I'm on, but also because of the unexpected little detour on the drive here. Sucking his cock with my bare ass and pussy on display for anyone who might happen to wander by—even though we were in a deserted area and that was very unlikely—made me feel wanton and sexy. I still don't understand what it is about Maximus that makes me so willing to obey him completely when it comes to sexual acts, he just has that effect on me. When he turns those blue eyes on me and uses his growly, commanding voice, it's like he puts me under some kind of spell so I'm a helpless, dripping slave, desperate to please him however he desires.

By the time he returns, I've finished my gin and tonic. He's taken off his suit jacket and unbuttoned the top few buttons of his shirt. Just the glimpse of his muscular chest is enough to make me want to run my tongue along his skin.

"If you want to visit the ladies', now's the time," he tells me, pulling me to him and dropping a kiss on the side of my neck, where the tiny puncture wounds his fangs have made are still healing.

"I think I'd better," I say.

"Hurry."

Part of me is tempted to dawdle, to put off what's about to happen for as long as possible. But the other part of me just wants to get it over with.

Once I've peed, I wash my hands and reapply some lip gloss. My cheeks are stained pink and my eyes are glittering, highlighted by the bronze eyeliner I used to bring out the blue. Surprisingly, I don't look nearly as terrified as I feel, and I'm thankful for that.

Picking up my purse, I head out of the bathroom and back towards the bar.

To Maximus...

To my fate.

S *abina*

"Disrobe."

Maximus has a very distinct tone of voice when we play, and he's using it now. It's cold with just a hint of arrogance, and it twists my tummy into knots. It also makes me wet. Swallowing hard, I fumble to pull off my halter top, then unzip and slide my skirt down over my legs. As instructed, I'm not wearing any underwear, so simply removing those two items of clothing leaves me completely undressed. I can feel people's eyes on me as surely as if they were actually touching my skin but I force myself to ignore them. This is for Maximus. Any discomfort I experience now is for him. I need to keep reminding myself of that. Once I'm standing naked in front of him, he gestures to my shoes. "Those too."

I toe them off gratefully and push them aside, setting my clothes in a neat pile on top of them, out of the way.

"Kneel."

The floor is cold and hard against my shins, and I look up at him with my heart pounding, my mouth dry. I should have asked for some water. He's gazing down at me with a stern look on his face, but there's love in his eyes.

"Do you know why I'm about to punish you?"

I'm not sure whether he's talking so loudly just so I can hear him over the relentless pounding of the music, or so the people watching us can understand him too, but I don't care. I can feel my face heating up as the shame and guilt wash over me.

"Because I put myself in danger, Sir, disobeying you and worrying you."

"And you agree to this punishment?"

"Yes, Sir."

"Do you want it? Need it?"

"Yes, Sir."

"Ask for it."

Crap. This is the part I hate the most, I don't know why. "I'm so sorry I went behind your back and caused you so much worry," I manage. There's a sudden lump in my throat and I swallow past it, willing the tears pricking my eyes not to fall. I will not cry in front of all these people. Taking a deep breath, I continue. "I promise never to put you through anything like that again. Please punish me so that I can earn your forgiveness."

He looks down at me for a long moment, his expression unreadable. I resist the urge to wipe my sweaty palms on my thighs.

"Very well. You may stand."

He reaches down to help me to my feet, and I look beyond him to the play area he's set up.

It's the one on the far left along the wall, and it currently holds an adjustable table like the ones people might use for massages. Different parts of it can be raised, but right now they're all level. I don't see any restraints or implements; just his toybag on the adjacent table, and my roses lying beside it. More people have appeared to watch my public humiliation; more people I studiously ignore.

"Spread your legs a little. Hands behind your back."

Even though it's warm down here in the club, my nipples are already taut and I'm turned on despite—or because of—the situation I'm in. I do as I'm told.

"Close your eyes."

I obey, and a moment later, there's the snap of a rubber glove, and the familiar smell of Tiger Balm reaches my nostrils. I know where it's going before he applies it: a generous dollop right on my already throbbing clit. It feels good as he slathers it over my swollen little nubbin, and I moan.

"Turn around and bend over."

I'm only just able to stop myself from protesting. Holding my tongue, I do so, and when he instructs me to spread my ass cheeks, I obey, my face as hot as the fire which is about to engulf my most sensitive areas.

The balm on my clit is already beginning to tingle as he spreads some more onto my most private hole, and I bite my lip hard as he slides his fingertip inside, making sure I'll be feeling the heat both inside and out. I'm unable to stop another moan from escaping my lips.

There's the snap of him removing his glove. "Good girl. Now, straighten up, and go and get your roses."

I walk gingerly to the table, wondering what on earth he has planned. Tiger Balm is a cunning trick; it has a hot sting to it which never fails to make my pussy wet, which in turn increases the burn. Even though I pick the flowers up carefully, a thorn pricks my finger.

"Lay them on the table right there. Horizontally." He points to a spot on the bench at about hip height, and I realize with horror what he has planned.

It's devious, sadistic and evil. It's also impressively creative. And if I wasn't being punished right now, I would tell him so.

Once the roses are in place, he orders me to get up and lie face-down on the table. I clamber up, and hesitate once I'm on my hands and knees. If I lie down flat, the thorny stems will be pressed directly against my hips—and my mons.

"You don't have to put your weight on your lovely flowers if you don't want to," he says, and I can hear the smugness in his voice. "If you can manage to hold your hips off them for the duration of your punishment, you're welcome to do so."

I hear a chuckle from someone in the crowd, and close my eyes. The burn of the Tiger Balm is still increasing, surely it must reach its peak soon? The very air on my pussy lips as I move serves to remind me how wet I already am.

With extreme caution, I lower myself to my elbows and wiggle my knees back until I'm as close to lying flat as possible while still keeping my pelvis above the thorny stems of the roses. It's a strenuous position to maintain, and I wonder how long I'll have to hold it for.

"Feel free to drop down if you like," Maximus says, "that's up to you. You're getting fifty with the birch."

Closing my eyes, I let out a moan of horror. I loathe and detest any implement which stings, and the birch is one of my pet hates—a fact Maximus is all too aware of.

"Seeing as you're not in the most comfortable of positions, I'll make it as quick as I can," he goes on, and I can't decide whether that's a good thing or not. "But you've earned this punishment, Sabina, and I want to make sure you really learn your lesson."

Truth be told, I've already learned it. Every moment of this scenario from the minute we reached the scene area was designed to cause me maximum humiliation and discomfort, but I will see this through if it kills me.

When I feel the water spray hitting my butt and thighs, I begin to think that maybe it actually *will* kill me. This guy takes sadism to a whole other level. Under any other circumstances, I'd be *so* impressed. Right now, however, I'm just trying to decide whether to focus on the burning between my legs and asscheeks, the strain of holding my hips high enough so I don't get huge thorns plunged into my mound, or the fact that this is all happening in full view of a bunch of strangers.

Once Maximus has thoroughly drenched his target area, and water is trickling between my legs and running down over my hips, he leans down and murmurs in my ear. "You're being so brave, pet, I'm so proud of you. Be a good girl and take this for me."

His intoxicating scent reaches my nostrils and I inhale deeply, my heart fluttering at his proximity and praise. I would do anything for this man, I realize in that moment. "Yes, Sir."

"Are you ready to begin? You don't need to count them."

"Yes, Sir." My thighs are already shaking with the strain of holding myself up. I'm kicking myself for not doing my Pilates as diligently as I should have lately.

The birch is a deceptively quiet implement, and I don't hear the impact over the ambient noise, but my god, do I feel it. The bunch of whippy twigs thwacking my soaked, bare skin feels like a million bees stinging me, and Maximus wields it relentlessly in a punishing rhythm.

Over and over, he strikes my bare butt and the tops of my thighs, until my entire world has narrowed down to nothing but the sensations in my body between my belly button and my knees.

My entire body is trembling now, and I've forgotten to breathe. All I can do is grit my teeth as he delivers fifty brutal, stinging strokes at a lightning fast pace. The last three are full force, right on the crease where my buttocks meet my thighs, and I realize I'm howling at the top of my lungs.

"Hush, pet, it's all right, it's over." Maximus's voice sounds like it's coming from very far away, but it immediately soothes me. "I'm just taking away the roses now... there, you can drop your hips."

I don't even check to see whether the flowers are gone— the moment he says that, my pelvis hits the table. My ass and upper thighs are stinging so badly, I no longer feel the Tiger Balm.

"Just breathe, sweetheart. I need to wipe you down; you're bleeding."

I'm glad my face is buried in my forearms so nobody can see me grimace as he cleans my butt and the tops of my thighs with alcohol. It feels like he's pouring lemon juice into a million paper cuts, and I bite my lip to keep from screaming.

"There, baby, all done. You were so brave, I'm so proud of you."

"I'm so sorry, Sir," I whimper. Now that the pain is subsiding slightly, the emotional impact of the punishment is hitting me like a tsunami.

"Hush, it's over with now. I forgive you."

Those three little words are my undoing. I never cry from pain, but now my eyes are welling up with tears and I squeeze them shut, still hiding my face from the crowd.

"Spread your thighs for me."

My abused backside protests as I obey, sliding my legs as far apart as I can while still keeping my knees on the table.

"Good girl."

His fingertip on my ultra-sensitive clit makes me almost levitate off the bench, so sudden is the pleasure, so stark the contrast between agony and ecstasy.

"Do you want to come for me?" Without waiting for a reply, he slides two fingers deep inside my pussy. Pinning me down with his other arm across the small of my back, he finds my G-spot and rubs it so hard and fast that I climax almost instantly, squirting uncontrollably as he draws out my orgasm in that delicious, relentless way he has.

The fact that people are watching me lose control somehow only heightens my arousal and by the time he removes his fingers, I'm lying in a puddle of water and my own juice.

"Clean them."

My cheeks flaming, I realize he's holding his drenched digits in front of my mouth and I suck them obediently, tasting myself, keeping my eyes closed, and trying to pretend we're alone.

"Good girl. I'll give you a moment to recover while I get you cleaned up."

Moments later, I can feel him wiping me down with a washcloth and my heart melts at such a tender gesture from someone who also has such a sadistic and evil side. I lift my hips so he can slide a towel beneath me, and allow the endorphins to flood my body as I settle back down and close my eyes once more.

Despite the frankly still agonizing sting in my butt and thighs, I feel strangely content and comforted, as though a heavy weight has been lifted. At first, I think it's sheer relief that I survived the thing I had been dreading ever since Maximus first mentioned it yesterday, but then I realize it's more than that.

My heart feels lighter. Maximus has forgiven me for what I put him through but, perhaps more importantly, I've forgiven myself. I still feel regret, of course, and would behave differently if I could go back in time, but I no longer feel guilt. Nor do I feel sorry for Zeke. He was so ugly to me while we were alone in that clubhouse, I dread to think what might have happened had Maximus not come to my rescue. Maybe it's cold-hearted of me not to feel sad that he's dead, but at this point, I just feel relief that he's no longer a threat. He knew what Maximus is, and he knew what he was doing when he had his two friends tie me up and manhandle me into his car, essentially kidnapping me.

There are always consequences.

"Sabina?" Maximus's soft voice breaks into my thoughts. "Are you cold?"

It's then that I realize I'm shaking. "No. Endorphins," I tell him.

"Still, let's get you warm. Can you sit up?"

He helps me, and I wince as my well-striped butt takes my weight. Next moment, a thick, fluffy purple blanket is wrapped around my shoulders and I snuggle into it, gratefully accepting the bottle of water Maximus slides into my hand.

He really is wonderful at aftercare.

"How are you feeling?" Sitting down beside me, he wraps an arm around me and pulls me close, pressing a soft kiss to the top of my head.

"Strangely cleansed," I tell him. "Sore, of course, but good. You?"

"Incredibly, unbelievably proud," he says. "And impatient to get to the good part."

"The collaring?" I ask, suddenly realizing that I'd forgotten all about it. I'd been so focused on dreading the public punishment.

"And the thing that comes after that," he says, and I can hear the smile in his voice.

"Sex?"

"Feeding."

We both chuckle. It's the perfect opening to ask the question which has been weighing on me for a long time now. "You say Lucius turned you," I begin, already feeling him tense up against me. "Is it possible to turn me, too? I don't think I want to grow old and wrinkly while you stay this young and gorgeous."

"It is possible. It's dangerous and complicated, and it's a process rather than a one-time event, but it can be done," he says slowly. "But it's absolutely not a decision that should be entered into lightly, and I won't even entertain the thought of turning you until we've been together for at least a year."

"A year? That long?"

"Oh pet, a year is nothing when you're considering eternal life."

Suddenly I feel foolish. "Of course. Although I don't suppose *you* spent a year thinking about it."

He lets out a bark of laughter, but there's not much mirth behind it. "I wasn't really given a choice. I was almost dead when Lucius found me. If he hadn't begun the process right then and there..."

"You wouldn't be here with me today," I finish the sentence for him, surprised by the strength of the sorrow that thought brings me. "Remind me to thank Lucius someday."

"You can thank him in a minute," Maximus says. "He'll be down for the collaring."

"I'm nervous," I admit. "I was nervous before, and now it's even worse somehow."

His arm tightens around me and he presses another kiss to my hair. "The hard part is over with now, sweetheart. This is the part where I get to show everyone here just how much you mean to me. So, are you ready?"

"I assume I won't be allowed to get dressed again first?"

He chuckles, and this time there's genuine humor in it. "Nice try, pet. And you'll be losing the blanket, too."

"I figured as much. Oh well, I guess everyone here tonight has seen pretty much every square inch of me by now."

"Every beautiful, perfect square inch," Maximus corrects me. "Now, come on. Let's make this official."

M *aximus*

I COULDN'T BE MORE proud of Sabina, my stunning blonde girl with the Roman name, as she makes her way through the crowd, her hand tucked into my arm. Even though she's completely naked aside from her heels, which I allowed her to put back on, she's walking tall, showing no signs of discomfort or embarrassment.

She took her punishment with more courage than even I had anticipated. Fifty strokes of the birch on soaking wet skin left the entire area of her ass from the top of the crease, right down the backs of her thighs, crisscrossed with deep, scarlet cuts, some of which had already begun to bleed at around the halfway mark. She'll be feeling the effects of that whipping for quite some time, and even so, she's walking beside me as if she doesn't have a care in the world.

I feel as if my heart could explode with love. The rose

gold titanium chain bracelet is safely tucked in a box in my pants pocket, and I can't wait to lock it around her left wrist. I decided against a typical collar as I like her neck bare. Necklaces and collars only get in the way of choking, feeding, and other fun activities.

It's only a short walk from the play area to the dais, and I wanted to show her off—and her marks—so we took the long way around, making a full circuit of the dungeon. Now we're standing in front of the dais which holds Lucius and Selene's grand, imposing thrones.

If Lucius was surprised yesterday when I called him and said I might need him to perform a collaring this evening, he didn't show it. I was a bit worried he wouldn't be available at such short notice—after all, I didn't know for sure whether Sabina would say yes until seven o'clock—but he'd merely chuckled. "We go back a long way," he'd said, "and it's been so many years since I last saw you this happy. Of course, I'd be honored to preside over the ceremony."

The king and queen of Toxic are seated in their places of honor now, both looking glamorous and regal, as always. Selene's eyes are glittering with amusement and I know why: she's often teased me about never wanting to settle down.

In this instance, I don't mind being wrong.

Lucius rises as we approach the dais, and I incline my head respectfully. Sabina does the same.

"Maximus," he says, his voice carrying across the room. "Is this the girl you would like to own?"

"Indeed, sire," I say, using my most formal way of addressing him. The occasion warrants it. "This is Sabina."

"Very nice," Lucius replies. I can feel Sabina clutch my arm tighter. "Sabina, do you attest that you are here of your own free will, that you are entering into this agreement with

Maximus with a sound, clear mind, and full knowledge of what he will require of you?"

"I do, Sir." It's barely a whisper, but I know Lucius heard it all the same.

"Then I give you both my blessing."

"Thank you, sire," I tell him. Then I slide Sabina's hand out from the crook of my elbow, turn her so that we're facing each other, and tell her to kneel. She does so without hesitation and once again, a wave of pride fills my chest.

"Sabina," Lucius says. "Do you promise to love, serve, and obey Maximus in all things as your dominant, in the knowledge that he will love, protect, and respect you in return, never asking anything of you that would cause you harm?"

This time, Sabina's reply is clear as a bell. Her lovely blue eyes are glistening with tears as she gazes up at me. "I promise."

"And you, Maximus," Lucius continues, "in return for her submission and devotion, do you swear to love, cherish and protect Sabina in all things, and promise never to willfully cause her harm?"

"I swear it," I say, pulling the black box out of my pocket and opening it to remove the bracelet.

"Let this jewelry be a symbol of the promises you made to one another this night," Lucius goes on, "as well as a mark of ownership. Maximus, you may proceed."

"Give me your left wrist, pet," I tell Sabina, and she raises her hand obediently. The titanium chain fits perfectly and as I put it on her, I thank the gods for sending me such a wonderful woman. I never thought I'd feel love like this again, and it's only now that I'm realizing how much I missed it. Craved it. "Do you like it?" I whisper once I've locked the bracelet securely around her wrist, and Sabina nods, even though she's barely looked at it.

"Read the inscription on the pendant," I tell her, and she does so, giving a little gasp of pleasure. "And the other side." I had a rose gold pendant added to the bracelet, and I had it engraved. On one side, in a delicate, slanted script, it reads: *Maximus.* On the other: *Cherished pet.*

"I love you, Sir," she says, and the tear sliding down her cheek is almost my undoing.

"I love you. You may stand."

I had almost forgotten where we were until I hear the spontaneous round of applause as Sabina gets carefully to her feet. Pulling her against me, I tug her head back and kiss her on and on, trying to convey without words what I feel for her.

"Congratulations, you two." Lucius's bemused voice interrupts our passionate embrace. "Now for gods' sake, get a room." There's a ripple of laughter, but it's good-natured.

"I need to be alone with you now," I tell Sabina, running a finger down her cheek.

"Sounds good to me, Sir," she replies.

"And as it happens, I know just the place." I take her hand and lead her to the back of the dungeon, to the private play booths. Originally I had intended to take her home, to my place, to consummate our new commitment to one another there. But now I realize I simply cannot wait that long. Even though she made me come so intensely earlier this evening, I've been hard as granite since I first made her get up on that table, and it's time to take her in the one place I haven't yet.

Before daybreak, Sabina will be mine in every way possible.

Sabina

Everything feels so surreal, it's like I'm in a dream. If it is, I never want to wake up. As I knelt before Maximus and he locked that gorgeous bracelet around my wrist to symbolize his ownership of me, I thought I might explode with joy. And the expression on his handsome face when he helped me back to my feet... nobody's ever looked at me with so much love before.

Maybe I can take care of myself, maybe I am strong and independent, but I no longer want to be. I want to lean on him. I welcome his protection. I love him.

"I'm so hungry for you," he growls as soon as we enter the booth. It's the one we first played in. It feels like we've come full circle. "Come here."

I go to him willingly, relishing the feel of his lips and tongue on my neck, my breasts, my belly. He cups my abused butt, squeezing the cheeks roughly, renewing the sting, and I mewl with pain. Then his mouth finds mine and he kisses me as I unbutton his shirt, suddenly desperate to feel his skin under my fingertips. I want to be closer to him than ever before.

His tongue is exploring my mouth as he unbuckles his belt, unbuttons and unzips his pants, and shoves them to his ankles before stepping out of them. "Gods, you taste so good," he groans, and I'm vaguely aware of him kicking off his shoes. "Play with my cock."

I don't need to be told twice. I take his rigid length in my hand, closing my fist around it and stroking it slowly, wanting to tease and torment him the way he does me. He groans against my lips, and his fingers slide between my thighs and find my clit.

He washed off the Tiger Balm when he cleaned me earlier after my punishment, but the whole area is still throbbing and incredibly sensitive, and I gasp when he begins to stroke my taut little nubbin with deft, precise movements designed to drive me insane.

"I'm so proud of you," he murmurs in between kisses, "and it was so hot to watch you squirt everywhere in front of all those people like a wanton little slut."

He knows exactly what his dirty talk does to me and it has the desired effect: a little gush of liquid heat floods his hand. "I bet most of them want to fuck you, but you know I'm the only one who gets to do that. You're mine now."

"Yours," I moan as he strokes me faster.

"Now," he growls, and I go over the edge, waves of pleasure washing over my whole body. I'm still moaning and shuddering as he spins me around, bends me over the nearest table, and plunges his huge cock deep inside my fluttering pussy. His pelvis smacking against my stinging butt only serves to heighten the pleasure.

"I love your tight little cunt," he says, gripping my hips so hard that I know he'll leave bruises. "I love the way it clamps down on my cock when you come. I love how wet I can make you, how fucking responsive you are."

All I can do is gasp as he pounds into me with a ferocity which takes my breath away. It feels so good, I never want him to stop.

"But there's still one place I haven't been," he continues, and the next moment, I feel his fingertip stroking my most private hole. "I'm going to fuck you here, pet," he growls. "It's going to stretch you, and it's going to hurt, and you're going to come harder than you ever thought possible."

The mere threat is enough to drive me to the brink. "Please," I gasp, fighting to hold back. "Please may I come?"

"No. Not until I'm deep in here." He slides his finger into my back channel then, and I yelp as the ring of muscle clamps down in protest. "You need to relax, pet."

I've done anal before, but never with anyone so big. "I'm scared, Sir," I admit, then jump when he bends down and kisses my back.

"Do you trust me, sweetheart?"

"Yes, Sir."

"Then just breathe and let me do this." He removes his finger and I hear a click. The next moment, something thick and cool is being dribbled between my asscheeks. Lube.

Just as he did with the Tiger Balm earlier, he slathers a good amount of it on and around my back hole and then inserts one finger. It slides in more easily this time, and I groan as he begins to work it in and out.

"Gods, you're tight," he says. "I'm not gonna last long."

After giving one more hard thrust inside my pussy, he withdraws his cock and removes his finger at the same time. I feel suddenly, achingly empty.

"Just getting myself ready," he says, and I can hear the wet sound of him slathering lube over his cock. "Turn around and get up on the table," he orders, and I do as he says. "Lie back. I want your ass hanging over the edge."

He looks so handsome standing there naked, stroking his impressive erection, the muscles of his chiseled chest gleaming in the low light.

"All right, pet, I need you to relax as much as possible. Let me help you." I watch him as he reaches between my spread legs, and moan as his lubed finger finds my clit. He's stroking tantalizing circles around it with one hand, and lining up his cock at my back entrance with the other. "Put your ankles on my shoulders, there's a good girl."

I force myself to focus on the sensations he's creating in my swollen bud as the broad, blunt head of his cock begins to press against my most tight hole.

"Bear down as I enter you," he orders, and I let out a yelp of pain as he pushes himself in slowly, inch by agonizing inch. As much as I want to, it's impossible to do what he asks and push back. He applies a little more pressure to my clit and I groan, another orgasm building despite—or maybe because of—the ache in my back channel.

"You're doing so good, baby," he murmurs, "I'm so proud of you. Almost there. You can take it, just focus on this..." He gives my clit a quick, hard pinch before resuming the relentless stroking, and my wiggle of pleasure helps him slide even further inside me.

I feel like I'm being torn in half but another part of me is relishing all of it, even the pain.

"So fucking tight," he groans, and then he delivers another pinch as he slides all the way home. I let out a howl.

"Better get used to it, pet," he tells me as he begins to move in short, gentle digs, only withdrawing an inch or two before sliding back in. "I plan to use this hole often, and thoroughly. And you're gonna learn to love it."

I'm on fire in more ways than one, and even though my ass is stretched to the point of pain, my clit is pounding like a drum beneath his expert fingertip.

"How long we do this for is up to you, pet," Maximus continues, still thrusting in and out of my burning back hole, slowly increasing the depth of his thrusts. "I'm not gonna stop until you come with my cock in your ass."

Again, his words make me gush, proof of my arousal

slipping out of my pussy and sliding down to add to the lube coating his erection.

"And then, when you're coming nice and hard for me," he continues, stroking my rigid clit faster now, "I'm gonna fill this tight little hole with my cum as I plunge my teeth into your neck and push your orgasm to heights you never even imagined."

Maximus is as good as his word. That last threat sends me over the edge and I climax beneath his fingertip, shuddering as he draws it out for several delicious seconds, before coming himself with a guttural shout. I can feel his cock jerking inside my ass as he leans down, forcing himself in deeper as my knees are pushed to my chest, and sinking his fangs into my neck as he begins to feed...

It's the most intense thing I've ever experienced and as I lie quaking on the table, wave after wave of orgasmic pleasure originating in my clit and spreading through my entire body, Maximus's seed filling my ass as he pumps my neck full of pleasure venom, my heart is overflowing with love, and I know without a doubt that this is where I belong.

With my vampire master.

Forever.

∼

WANT MORE MIDNIGHT DOMS?

Click here to sign up for news!

Read the whole series for more of your favorite vampire BDSM club:

Alpha's Blood by Renee Rose & Lee Savino

Her Vampire Master by Maren Smith

Her Vampire Prince by Ines Johnson

Her Vampire Hero by Nicolina Martin

Her Vampire Bad Boy by Brenda Trim

Her Vampire Rebel by Zara Zenia

Her Vampire Obsession by Tymber Dalton, writing as Lesli Richardson

Her Vampire Temptation by Alexis Alvarez

Her Vampire Addiction by Tabitha Black

Coming soon...

Her Vampire Lord by Ines Johnson

ALSO BY TABITHA BLACK

ABOUT THE AUTHOR

USA Today bestselling author Tabitha Black has been writing erotic romance for well over a decade, mostly in the age-play and historical genres. More recently, she's discovered the joys of writing more contemporary books with a greater emphasis on BDSM, as well as darker, edgier fiction. Her latest foray is into the fascinating world of M/f Omegaverse, although she has always had a soft spot for vampires.

Having lived in four countries on three different continents, she likes to "write to discover what she knows."

She has a weakness for great lattes, strong, alpha men, and tattoos.

Tabitha loves getting mail, so if you want to drop her a line, please do so at tabitha_black@hotmail.com. Subscribe to her newsletter to be the first to hear about new releases! You can also follow her on Amazon, BookBub, and/or join her Facebook page. Thank you for reading!